RT Bc  Presents: The Haunted West

Volume One

Heather Graham

Katherine Neville

Bobbi Smith

Tina Wainscott

Jennifer St. Giles

Kat Martin

Tina DeSalvo

Richard Devin

Lance Taubold

Featuring a bonus story from RT BookLovers 2018 contest winner

Charissa Weaks

All rights reserved.
This is a work of fiction. Any similarities between real life events and people, and the events within this product are purely coincidental.

13Thirty Books
Print and Digital Editions
Copyright 2018

Discover new and exciting works by 13Thirty Books at
www.13thirtybooks.com

Print and Digital Edition, License Notes

This print/ebook is licensed for your personal enjoyment only. This print/ebook may not be re-sold, bartered, barrowed or loaned to others. Thank you for respecting the work of this and all 13Thirty Books authors.

DEDICATION

Thank you RT for making the romance industry what it is today. RT is truly the luminary of the industry.

Thank you Kathryn, Carol, Ken, Jo Carol, Kate, and all the RT staff for your perseverance, dedication, guidance, and ingenuity, which knows no bounds.

CONTENTS

FOREWORD

Diana Gabaldon

I grew up in the West and–aside from a brief and horrible eighteen months on the east coast (major culture shock)–have always lived here. My old family home is in Flagstaff, at the foot of an extinct volcano that is a sacred mountain to at least thirteen local Native American tribes, including the Hopi and the Navajo (to whom it 's Dook 'o 'ooslííd, the sacred mountain of the west, built with pieces of abalone shell brought from the Third World).

Out beyond the mountains, on the high desert near Sunset Crater, are the ruins of Wupatki and Wukoki, built more than a thousand years ago by people we call the Sinagua or Anasazi, because they are lost, along with their names. I've sat (a long time ago, lest the National Park Service become Concerned…) on a wall at Wupatki by the light of a full moon and listened to the earth breathe, through blowholes from the caves below. I mean, you want to talk haunted?

And then to the south, among the low deserts and their mountains and mirages, we have the stories of lost miners, cowboys and desperate gun-slingers: think the OK Corral, Wyatt Earp and Doc Holiday, Boot Hill and Tombstone (one of my grandfathers was at one time editor of *The Tombstone Epitaph*, the town 's newspaper, which I thought was pretty neat). There's even an official ghost-town–Jerome, in the Mingus Mountains, a (mostly) abandoned mining town–though there are a lot of less-known places in the

Southwest where people have once lived… and maybe still do, though their earthly traces have vanished.

And that's just Arizona.

What I mean is, you could hardly find more fertile ground than the West, if what you want is a peek through the veil between this world and… others.

The stories in this book are a fascinating array of paranormal suspense, romance, and mystery, where parted lovers find each other on the other side of death and the spirits of dead killers still roam among the living. If love never dies… does evil?

In a long life of walking battlefields and ferreting through the past, I've often sensed Things—everyone does, I think. Nobody visits Culloden without feeling the presence of its dead. I've been in a lot of very old places, from Scotland to the Sonoran desert, and if you sit still and listen, you definitely get Echoes. But in terms of specific, individual, *personal* ghosts… I've met only three. I mean, I don't go *looking* for ghosts—I wouldn't recommend it; people tend to find things they go looking for—but now and again…

All three of these encounters happened in western settings, interestingly enough. I say "encounters" because I luckily don 't *see* ghosts; I know people who do and they mostly don't like it. I just… know they 're there, just as I'd know someone was in the room with me, even if I had my eyes closed.

Speaking of eyes closed…

One gentleman—I knew he was male—tried to get in bed with me at a conference hotel in Snowbird, Utah, of all unlikely places to be haunted. I was lying on my side, settling slowly toward sleep, when I felt the mattress give behind me, and someone lay down and put his arm around me. My initial drowsy thought was that it was my husband… and then I realized he wasn't with me; I was alone. Or supposed to be alone.

I flipped onto my back, blinking at the dark, and turned on the light. Nothing. Orderly, clean, impersonal hotel room. OK, I often see random things in my mind 's eye when drifting off to sleep… turned off the light, settled down again. And it happened again. Only I wasn't anywhere *near* asleep that time.

"Hey!" I said. "You stop that! I'm married!" Got up, turned on the light, fetched my rosary from my bag and put it down on the empty (well, "empty") side of the bed, then cautiously lay down again, one eye open, as it were. He seemed to have got the message, though, and didn't come back.

Another ghost was more recent, a couple of years ago. It wasn't a conscious encounter–I knew she was there, but she didn't sense me–but was disturbing. I 'd stopped at a roadside rest stop, on my way from Phoenix to Flagstaff, in the evening, and when I walked in, the women 's restroom was empty (unusual; it's a busy rest-stop). I pushed open the door of a cubicle, and walked straight into this woman. I couldn't see her, but dang, she was there.

She was relatively young and she was a mess, flailing and throwing herself at the walls. My best guess is that she 'd died in there of something like a drug overdose; she was bleary and incoherent, and definitely didn't know I was there. I backed straight out, of course, stood there (as one does) blinking for a few moments, then cautiously stuck my head back into the cubicle. Still there, an atmosphere of frenzy and despair. Really squalid way to go, poor thing.

I don 't set up to be an exorcist–like I say, I don 't go looking for these things–but the *only* thing I could do in the circumstances was to take a deep breath, step back inside and say a prayer for the peace of her soul. I mean, how can you leave somebody trapped in a public toilet without at least trying? So I did, and then stepped out, chose a different cubicle, and then left. I don 't know if she's still there or not; I haven 't gone back to look. I don 't want to meet her again, if she is.

The first ghost I met, though, was something quite different. It happened–reasonably enough–in the Alamo, in San Antonio. This was in 1990 or 91, just before OUTLANDER was released. I was attending a conference of the Romance Writers of America (or possibly the *Romantic Times* Convention, I forget) at the Menger Hotel, which is an old place, right across the street from the Alamo, which now stands in a small botanical park.

A friend had driven up from Houston to see me, and he suggested that we go walk through the Alamo, he being a botanist and therefore interested in the plants outside. He also thought I might find the building interesting. He said he 'd been there several times as a child, and had found it "evocative." So we strolled through the garden, looking at ornamental cabbages, and then went inside.

The present memorial is the single main church building, which is essentially no more than a gutted masonry shell. There's nothing at all in the church proper–a stone floor and stone walls, bearing the marks of hundreds of thousands of bullets; the stone looks chewed. There are a couple of smaller semi-open rooms at the front of the church, where the baptismal font and a small chapel used to be; these are separated from the main room by stone pillars and partial walls.

Around the edges of the main room are a few museum display cases, holding such artifacts of the defenders as the Daughters of Texas have managed to scrape together–rather a pitiful collection, including spoons, buttons, and (scraping the bottom of the barrel, if you ask me) a diploma certifying that one of the defenders had graduated from law school (this, like a number of other artifacts there, wasn't present in the Alamo during the battle, but was obtained later from the family of the man to whom it belonged).

The walls are lined with execrable oil paintings, showing the various defenders in assorted "heroic" poses. I suspect them all of having been executed by the Daughters of Texas in a special arts-and-crafts class held for the purpose, though I admit that I might be maligning the D of T by this supposition. At any rate, as museums go, this one doesn't.

It is quiet–owing to the presence of a young woman waving a "Silence, Please! THIS IS A SHRINE!" sign in the middle of the room– but is not otherwise either spooky or reverent in atmosphere. It's just a big, empty room. My friend and I cruised slowly around the room, making *sotto voce* remarks about the paintings and looking at the artifacts.

And then I walked into a ghost. He was near the front of the main room, about ten feet in from the wall, near the smaller room on the left (as you enter the church). I was surprised by this encounter, since a) I 'd never met a ghost before; b) I hadn't expected to meet a ghost right then, and c) if I had, he wasn't what I would have expected.

I saw nothing, experienced no chill or feeling of oppression or malaise. The air felt slightly warmer where I stood, but not so much as to be really noticeable. The only really distinct feeling was one of… communication. Very distinct communication. I *knew* he was there–and he certainly knew *I* was. It was the feeling you get when you meet the eyes of a stranger and know at once this is someone you'd like.

I wasn't frightened in the least; just intensely surprised. I had a strong urge to continue standing there, "talking" (as it were; there were no words exchanged then) to this–man. Because it *was* a man; I could "feel" him distinctly and had a strong sense of his personality. I rather naturally assumed that I was imagining this, and turned to find my friend, to re-establish a sense of reality. He was about six feet away, and I started to walk toward him. Within a couple of feet, I lost contact with the ghost; couldn't feel him anymore. It was like leaving someone at a bus stop; a sense of broken communication.

Without speaking to my friend, I turned and went back to the spot where I had encountered the ghost. There he was. Again, he was quite conscious of me, too, though he didn't say anything in words. It was a feeling of "Oh, there you are!" on both parts.

I tried the experiment two or three more times–stepping away and coming back–with similar results each time. If I moved away, I couldn't feel him; if I moved back, I could. By this time, my friend was becoming understandably curious. He came over and whispered, "Is this what a writer does?", meaning to be funny. Since he evidently didn't sense the ghost–he was standing approximately where I had been–I didn't say anything about it, but merely smiled and went on outside with him, where we continued our botanical investigations.

The whole occurrence struck me as so very odd–while at the same time feeling utterly "normal"–that I went back to the Alamo–alone, this time–on each of the next two days. Same thing; he was there, in the same spot, and he knew me. Each time, I would just stand there, engaged in what I can only call mental communication. As soon as I left the spot–it was an area maybe two to three feet square–I couldn't sense him anymore.

I did wonder who he was, of course. There are brass plates at intervals around the walls of the church, listing the vital statistics of all the Alamo defenders, and I'd strolled along looking at these, trying to see if any of them rang a psychic bell, so to speak. None did.

Now, I did mention the occurrence to a few of the writers at the conference, all of whom were very interested. I don't think any of them went to the Alamo themselves–if they did, they didn't tell me–but more than one of them suggested that perhaps the ghost wanted me to tell his story, I being a writer and all. I said dubiously that I didn't *think* that's what he wanted, but the next–and last–time I went to the Alamo, I did ask him, in so many words.

I stood there and thought–consciously, in words–" What do you want? I can't really do anything for you. All I can give you is the knowledge that I know you're there; I care that you lived and I care that you died here."

And he *said*–not out loud, but I heard the words distinctly inside my head; it was the only time he spoke–he said, "That's enough."

At once, I had a feeling of completion. It *was* enough; that's all he wanted. I turned and went away. This time, I took a slightly different path out of the church, because there was a group of tourists in my way. Instead of leaving in a straight line to the door, I passed around the pillar dividing the main church from one of the smaller rooms. There was a small brass plate in the angle of the wall there, not visible from the main room.

The plate said that the smaller room had been used as a powder magazine during the defense of the fort. During the last hours of the siege, when it became apparent that the fort would fall, one of the defenders had made an effort to blow up the magazine, in order to destroy the fort and take as many of the attackers as possible with it. However, the man had been shot and killed just outside the smaller room, before he could succeed in his mission–more or less on the spot where I met the ghost.

So, I don 't know for sure; he didn't tell me his name, and I got no clear idea of his appearance–just a general impression that he was fairly tall; he spoke "down" to me, somehow. But for what it's worth, the man who was killed trying to blow up the powder magazine was named Robert Evans; he was described as being "black-haired, blue-eyed, nearly six feet tall, and always merry." That last bit sounds like the man I met, all right, but there's no telling.

Oddly enough, I did write about this man, indirectly. In *DRUMS OF AUTUMN*, a woman who's had an accident and found herself stranded in the wilderness overnight meets the ghost of an Indian, and… well, if Robert Evans is indeed the gentleman I met, I imagine he might find it entertaining.

I can't say how many–if any–of the unearthly encounters in this diverse collection might be based on some experience of the authors, or whether they derive purely from the realms of imagination. But I *can* say they're entertaining. Hope you enjoy them all!

–Diana Gabaldon

1

FREE MY SOUL

Tina Wainscott

Lorna Meyers had lived many lives, had many passionate romances, and just as many happily-ever-afters. She then left them behind when she finished the last edit and sent her manuscript through cyberspace to her publisher. There was one life, however, that she wasn't able to leave—her own. She had fortune, yes, and the kind of fame a bestselling author can have, toiling away alone most of the time with brief spots of stardom at a book signing or television interview. And here especially at the RT Booklover's Convention, where readers gushed over her words and stood in long lines to buy her books at the huge signing event. Yes, she had that, but it didn't fill the yawning chasm inside her. Each book became harder to write, harder to find that something fresh and exciting for her.

She had even once entertained the thought of ending it. Not just her career either. The notion would flit into her mind. When she'd spot a high rooftop. Or a sharp bend in the road. Sometime she'd even imagine—she did have an excellent imagination, after all—the headlines as her favorite *Good Morning America* anchor reported the tragic news, showing a clip of their last interview. Lorna would never do it, of course, but the idea that she fantasized about it did worry her.

The annual convention always revived her spirits and gave her a much-needed boost. Except for all the many new rising stars crowding into the field, vying to outshine her star. Younger, thinner, more media savvy, pumping out up to six books a year to stay "discoverable." She, at the age of forty-two, was considered slow, old, and probably outdated. It was only a matter of time.

Lorna often went on a self-driven tour of the convention city so she could use it for research. She'd never set a book in Reno before, and her early research had her accidentally clicking on the Red Velvet Inn's site. Or maybe not so accidentally. From the moment she saw the picture of the historic building that had once been a bordello, an overwhelming feeling of familiarity beset her. Joy and grief twisted around her like a vine, urging her fingers to click on each page on the site and soak in the description and black-and-white pictures.

Why the intense fascination? She didn't even write historical romance, nor did she read much of it. But something tugged and taunted and, before she knew it, she'd made a reservation to stay there.

Now, she stood at the entrance of a four-story brick building that looked like an aged grand-dame surrounded by slick, shiny millennials.

Like me.

Was that why she was so drawn to this place?

It was as though someone from behind nudged her toward the ornate wood door. She opened it and walked inside, only to be swept up in an even stronger sense of… belonging. Good Lord, had she been a prostitute in a former life? Did she even believe in such nonsense?

Certainly not.

To the right, a luxurious bar curved in a half-circle, befitting that decadent era. The lovingly scuffed high-backed stools and tarnished brass foot rails looked authentic. Of course, the maintenance department could have been just lazy. A couple sat at one end, a lone man in the middle.

To the left, a glass door announced the office and check-in. She strayed, though, to the framed photographs on the walls, many of the same pictures she'd seen on the website. This had clearly been an elegant bordello, if one could think such a thing. The women were beautiful and classy, with none of the desperate sadness she'd have expected on their faces.

Other than her own reflection in the glass, she mused.

She felt no sense of having been or known the people in the

pictures. But the familiarity of this place pervaded her very being. And the tug continued to pull her further back into the lobby. She smelled freshly cut wood and plaster and paint, though she could see no sign of construction.

She was drawn to a glass case almost as tall as she. A halogen light inside illuminated items from bygone eras. She felt silly as she again searched for some sense of personally having seen any of the items before. Then her gaze drew to a perfume bottle made of opalescent glass in an odd shade of orange-pink. Its shape reminded her of a woman's curves, its "skin" etched in swirls.

Lorna *needed* to touch the decanter. Unfortunately, a small brass sign on the door read *DO NOT OPEN*. There, it was settled.

But, in fact, it wasn't. The scent of construction grew stronger, mixed with a sweet rose perfume, though no one stood nearby. Since there was no liquid inside the bottle, no scent could be wafting out. The glass knob on the top was snugly in place—*tight, completely closed!*

Whose voice was that, speaking those fearful words in her mind? A character nudging into her consciousness?

She felt dizzy, maybe a little drunk. Had someone slipped something into her drink? But she hadn't had a drink yet. She tried to turn, to walk to the bar where she *could* have one and settle her nerves. But she couldn't move, nor could she tear her eyes from that bottle. Suddenly she was opening the door, picking up the bottle that seemed to vibrate in her hands.

Wait. There *was* something inside the bottle. Not a liquid but a swirling... vapor?

Open, open, open, that voice that was not her own urged. She settled her fingers on the smooth glass ball on top.

"Put that down!"

Lorna broke out of the spell she'd been in, jerking around at the harsh male voice. Her hand hit the edge of the door, and the bottle fell. She and the man tried to grab for it, their hands collided, and the bottle bounced off them and hit the wood floor. The delicate glass shattered on impact.

The man grabbed her wrist. "What were you doing in the cabinet? You've broken it!" He stared at the bottle even as he yelled at her. What was he expecting it to do, instantly mend?

"I'm so sorry. I'll pay..." A rush of sound roared through her ears, accompanied by the perfume she'd smelled earlier. Words fled

3

her mind as dizziness overtook her. She stumbled back and fell into a wing chair.

It was as though she were looking through that glass; everything was distorted and tinted in that orange-pink color. She saw the man kneeling over the broken glass, then looking around him.

"I'm so very sorry," she tried again, feeling her thoughts start to coagulate. "I'll pay for it."

"She's gone," he murmured, his gaze on the bits of glass he gingerly picked up. He must have been very attached to the bottle. The man was probably around her age, handsome with dark hair and stormy blue eyes. But his sour disposition tainted his looks. "Leave," he gritted out.

Lorna started to rise. "I'm staying here. But you can charge my room for the piece. Or I'll search online for it. Do you have a picture, any information—" A surge of hatred washed over her at this man, so overwhelming that she stumbled back into the chair. *For* him, not from him. Sure, he was rude, but Lorna couldn't make sense of it. Following her instinct to get away from him, she stood and wheeled her luggage into the bar. She really needed a drink now.

Even better than a drink was the sight of the man behind the bar. Brown curls, cocoa-colored eyes full of warmth, and a surprised smile on his face as he looked in her direction. She glanced behind her, but no one stood there. She approached the bar, feeling as though she were seeing an old friend for the first time in years.

He met her at the place she'd chosen, his eyes taking her in. "You're back. It's you."

"I've never been here before in my life."

He narrowed his eyes, blinked. "Oh. My mistake."

I feel as though I've been here, she wanted to say. Something very strange was going on. As she opened her mouth, the man sitting three stools down smacked his empty mug on the countertop. "Where's the damn bartender in thish place?"

"Sir, that's rude. He's…" Before she could point him out, he silently shook his head, then disappeared around the back.

The man swiveled toward her. "Who're you?" He pointed at her. "*You're* rude."

"What are you, five years old?" she said in uncharacteristic confrontation.

The rude man maneuvered off the stool, fire in his eyes.

The man with the curls peered around the corner and nodded his chin for her to go. Then he tipped a bottle of whisky from the collection against the mirrored wall. It crashed on the floor, snagging the man's attention from her.

She snatched up her wheeled luggage and marched into the office. Goodness, what an odd place! Once she'd checked in and was given her brass key, she said, "There's a drunk man in the bar causing a scene. You might want to ask him to leave."

The friendly but harried-looking man whose nametag read *HARVEY* rolled his eyes. "Gus. I'm sorry about that. We try to keep him under-boozed."

She chuckled at the sentiment, and the phrase. "No need to apologize. The bartender was very nice. He created a diversion because the drunk man was about to get nasty with me." She didn't want to admit that the bartender had sacrificed a bottle of liquor to do it. Hopefully he'd cleaned it up.

"Our bartender went home sick about a half hour ago. In fact, I'm trying to cover for him when I can. Gosh, I hope a customer didn't go behind the bar." He darted out to the bar, where drunk Gus was stumbling out the front door.

Harvey checked behind the bar and then around that wall where the handsome man had ducked. He came back looking both relieved and puzzled. "No one back there. Um, can you describe the man you saw?"

"Sure. I'll probably sound like a romance author, but he was tall, with wide shoulders, lean. His eyes were warm and loving, like you could tell him all your woes or, just as easily, lean forward and kiss him. He had a square jaw and a full mouth, and his curls were tempting my fingers to dive in."

"You saw him, then?"

"Saw… him? Well, yes." Trying to sound casual and not overly eager or curious, she said, "Who is he?"

"Nate Hawkins," the manager said with a slow nod.

Nate. She rolled the name around in her head, but it echoed deep in her heart instead. "I'd love to, uh, meet him."

Harvey mulled her request over, glanced around, then subtly waved her closer. "Come with me."

Perhaps Nate was in some other role and had been merely standing behind the bar. She didn't know why she was even asking

5

for him. He was a bit too young for her. Too handsome, for sure. God, he could be married for all she knew, or attached, or gay or…

She'd followed the manager into a back office and pointed to a color picture on the wall. "Is this who you saw?"

"Yes!" She cleared her throat. *Too excited.* Remember the could be's. "That's him. He was very kind. Very chivalrous."

"And also very dead."

She stumbled back, as though the man had taken the framed picture off the wall and smacked her in the chest with it. "Pardon?"

"Nate Hawkins owned this place. Half of it, anyway. Here, take this out to the lobby and read it if you'd like. I have to call the plumber and raise some hell." He handed her a thin photo album and ushered her out.

Lorna heard the door click shut behind her but was too intent on the book in her hands. She found a blue velvet chair in the corner and sank down to it.

Inside were photos of Nate and others, covered in dust as they tore out chunks of drywall. Nate standing in front of the entrance with another man, holding huge scissors poised in front of a thick red ribbon. Beneath the photo someone had written "RE-OPENING DAY." She recognized the other man—the jerk who'd made her drop the bottle. The next page was the newspaper article about the hotel's restoration by new owners Nate Hawkins and Gerard Tate.

She turned the page, embarrassed to find her eyes drinking in Nate's face. She never felt the things her heroines felt. Every love scene, every flirtation, drawn from the books and movies she'd devoured as a young woman and writer… and her own fantasies. Her former fiancé was a handsome but cold man who rescued her from a dangerous home situation, then cheated on her at every opportunity. She'd escaped into romance novels, wishing and hoping and waiting for a man like the ones in those pages to rescue her. He never came, only toad after toad.

Then, by chance, she'd posted a "first meet" scene she'd written for fun to a writing forum, and an established author was impressed. She worked with Lorna, then introduced her to her agent. When Lorna quickly shot past that author, she was dumped as a protegee. And friend.

Lorna started viewing writing friendships dubiously. She kept her distance, part of the reason she never stayed at the conference hotel. She'd opted to room here to see if a story would come to her.

Her hero had come, in any case. But what was his story? She turned the page, and her idea of his HEA went to HELL. It was a newspaper article dated five years ago with the headline: *TRAGIC FIRE IN HISTORIC HOTEL KILLS TWO.*

Nate Hawkins and wife, Marina, were both burned beyond recognition when a fire ignited in their bedroom on the fourth floor of the Red Velvet Inn. Because of recent renovations to their residence, the window was blocked. It's not known whether the couple tried to open the door. Both were pronounced dead at the scene. The cause of the fire is still under investigation.

Lorna could not tear her gaze from the picture of Nate, smiling just as he'd been a short while ago at the bar. Finally, she shifted to the woman in the photo next to him, long dark hair with a smile as warm as his. Lorna's eyes tingled and her chest tightened, as though she too were in a room filled with smoke.

She turned the page, but there was no more news or pictures. Their story had ended.

Why did she feel that it hadn't?

Because Nate was still here.

Lorna walked back to the manager's office and knocked on the door, then entered. Still on the phone, he gave her a vague wave to indicate, *Go away, I'm busy, I'll talk to you later,* but she sat primly on the chair and continued looking at the album as he bitched at the man on the other end.

When he hung up, she asked, "Have others have seen him?"

"A few. The paranormal investigators call him a recording ghost. Meaning that his energy has imprinted here, that what they see is like a moment in time. He doesn't seem to see anyone or interact—"

"He interacted with me. He spoke to me."

"That would be a first, ma'am. I hope it wasn't too frightening"

"It wasn't frightening. It was…" *Touching. Startling. Moving.* "Interesting," she settled on. "Did you know him?"

Harvey smiled. "I worked with him at another hotel, and he brought me over. He was a great guy, fair, kind, as you said. When Nate died, Gerard inherited his half. It was hard enough to lose Nate and Marina. They were good people. Nate was a great boss. Gerard… well, he has a different management style."

"Asshole style." Lorna covered her mouth. "I can't believe I said that." She'd been raised to be polite, to stay silent if she had nothing nice to say.

Harvey lowered his voice when he said, "You would be correct, madam. Funny, that's something Marina would say. Had said, actually, in exactly those words."

Lorna's finger touched Nate's face beneath the film. It strayed to Marina. "What was she like?"

"Marina was an angel." He chuckled. "Until you crossed her or someone she cared about. Then she was all horns and fire. Once Mr. Tate lit into me for something I didn't do, and she got right up in his face and—"

A sharp knock on the door preceded Mr. Tate's barging in. "I want that cabinet out in the lobby locked. Some dumb cow just—" He saw her, and his phony smile looked more like a grimace. "Excuse us, ma'am."

She felt that fire Harvey had just spoken about rise up in her. But she had, after all, been in the wrong. "I suppose my being that cow might make it hard for you to speak your mind." With a snarky grunt, she left. Until she heard Tate yelling at the poor manager through the closed door. She opened it. "Stop yelling at Harvey! It wasn't his fault!" She met Tate's hard eyes with equal hardness, then snapped the door shut.

The adrenaline made her want to laugh, of all things. She went into the bar to look for Nate, but the place was empty. She needed more. More information. More... well, more Nate. Goodness, was she in love with a dead man she didn't even know?

You do know him.

That voice again. Maybe all of those imaginary people and situations had warped her brain. She headed to the relic elevator and went to her room. The accommodations were exquisite, with a lace comforter, high-end toiletries, and elegant wallpaper and curtains that evoked days gone by... but not so much the bordello aspect, thank goodness.

She fired up her laptop, signed into the hotel's WiFi, and started searching for follow-up articles about the fire. After reading employees' and guests' accolades about Nate's hospitality, and Marina's charm, Lorna found a later article titled *HISTORICAL HOTEL FIRE DEEMED ACCIDENTAL*. Investigators found a kerosene lamp, consistent with the era of the hotel, in the bedroom. The fire had quickly consumed the room and blocked the only exit. It was tragic timing, with the window being replaced the next day and Gerard Tate out of town and not in his own quarters to possibly help or at least call 911 earlier.

Tired from her trip, and the odd feelings coursing through her, she readied herself for bed. The convention started midday tomorrow, but she didn't usually attend the opening night mixer. All of that small talk, and no friends… it was excruciating.

She settled onto the bed, thinking about Nate and the fire. He'd died right here, one floor above. The thought gave her chills.

Half asleep, she smelled plaster again, and heard a woman laughing. "I'm not sure if that's an insult or a come on." Her voice was husky with a Spanish accent.

Then the fog parted, and the dream came fully alive. Nate stood a few feet away, his thumbs hooked into the belt loops of his well-worn jeans, his shirt and hair covered in dust. He had that warm smile with a dash of flirting. "It's neither, unless you want it to be a come on." He winked. "I'm just saying it's refreshing to see a woman doing gritty and dirty work. I wasn't saying that you were a dirty girl, but you do look intriguing covered in dust." He moved closer and plucked a small chunk of drywall from her long hair. "However, if you like being called a dirty girl, I'm all in." He held out his hand. "I'm Nate Hawkins."

She set down her big hammer and shook his hand. "Marina Gonzales." Lorna was seeing the scene through her eyes. Feeling Nate's calloused hand, his fingers wrapped around hers.

"Wait," she said. "You're one of the owners. Are you the one who's pretty much an a-hole?" She picked up the hammer and slung it against the drywall, breaking up another patch. "I don't want you thinking I'm slacking off or anything."

"No, I'm the nice one. Which is a good thing, since otherwise you'd have just called me an a-hole."

"Yeah, I guess I would have." Lorna could feel Marina's face scrunch up in a grimace. *Wow, this was so real.* Marina took out another section of old, crumbling drywall. "Glad it worked out the way it did."

"So far, anyway."

"Maybe I should keep my mouth shut, huh? I'm not so good at that, I have to warn you."

"I like the way you talk. Say whatever you want." He picked up a

9

nearby sledgehammer and crushed a nearby section of wall. "Like how god-awful this wallpaper is. Or maybe how foolish it is for a guy to go in on a hotel when he's never run one before."

"Foolish, no. Brave, bold, adventurous, yes. I'd love to own a place like this. My *abuela*, my grandmother, ran her own B&B in Mexico. She raised me when my mama died. I grew up in her B&B and pretty much did every job. Then she died."

"Why didn't you take it over?"

"Because it was her daughter's inheritance, and she was like your business partner. I used to call her a b-hole because her name is Bea. But I came here, and I enjoy this work. It's satisfying."

"But not as much as working at the B&B," Nate said with a knowing smile.

"No."

Lorna felt her sadness, the loss.

"Maybe you could work here. Some of the former hotel's employees have moved on. Obviously they couldn't stay unemployed while we renovated this place. We're keeping Harvey on as the night manager, but we'll have a lot of opportunities."

Now Marina's excitement flooded through Lorna. "Let's talk about possible positions. I mean, employment positions," she added quickly, though Lorna could hear her thoughts: *Maybe I am a dirty girl, 'cause that's not what I was thinking!*

Lorna woke with a start. What a crazy, vivid dream.

Or was it?

She threw on her clothes and went downstairs to find Harvey.

He was fastening a cable tie around the handles on the case. "You look like you've seen a ghost. Have you?"

"I wish. I mean, I confess I'm fascinated with recent history here."

"You mean with Nate."

She sighed. *Might as well admit it.* "Yes, and with Marina as well. How did they meet?"

He tested the handles, and the tie held. "She was working with the construction company during the renovations."

Her heart squeezed tight. "Doing drywall, by chance?"

"Yes, really a little of everything. Nate was very hands on, so they met during the reno and fell in love."

Love. Lorna felt it sweep through her. That and the realization that she hadn't had a dream about their first meeting—*she'd relived it.* "Thank you, Harvey." She started back to her room but stopped. "Does anyone live in their old apartment? I'd love to see it."

"You, madam, are becoming a little obsessed. But no, you cannot see it. It hasn't been completely repaired yet. No guests are allowed up there as it's dangerous. And don't get any ideas. Mr. Tate resides in the other half of the fourth floor. If he catches you…" Harvey shrugged. She knew how he'd be.

The rules, who cares about them?

Marina. That was something she'd say; Lorna was sure about that.

But how?

It was as inexplicable as the knowledge that she would, in fact, go up to the apartment. She took the stairs, only momentarily deterred by the chain across the steps to the fourth level with the sign that read *PRIVATE RESIDENCE.* Technically, it didn't say not to enter. Right?

Feeling a surge of brazenness that was so unlike her, she continued up and quietly opened the door. The hallway looked somewhat like the level her room was on, only more faded and dusty. It hit her that she didn't know which of the two doors had belonged to Marina and Nate, then she walked directly to the one on the left and tried the knob. It turned easily, and she walked into the empty space. It had been renovated, at least to the point of the walls being drywalled and baseboard installed. Faint scents of both smoke and plaster wafted through, but she saw no sign of the blaze. It had to have been terrifying. That was something she surely didn't want to dream about. Or relive rather.

Relive?

Before she could ponder the odd word she'd chosen, the hairs on the back of her neck jumped to attention. She spun around and saw a man standing a couple of yards away. For a second she feared she'd been caught by Mr. Tate, but no, Nate stood there.

You're back. It's you. That's what he'd said before.

Now he just took her in with a curious smile.

"Nate," she said, and it came out in a husky whisper. She felt a rush of affection for this man who was not only a stranger but… dead.

"How much do you know?" he asked.

11

"I know that you died here in a fire."

"So they say."

"You're not dead?" She wanted it to be so.

"Alas, I am. And what about you?"

"I've been dead... on the inside for a long time. God, I've missed you." Lorna slapped her hand over her mouth. "I don't know why I said that!"

He took a step closer, his head tilted. "But you do. Think about it. Or feel about it. I mean, go within and ask yourself what's going on."

Lorna's hand slid to her throat. "I'm so confused. Everything that's happened since I came here has been surreal."

"Tell me." He seemed to hang on her every word.

"I felt drawn to this place, the very moment I saw it on the Internet. And when I walked in, it felt so familiar. I was drawn to a bottle in the glass case just off the lobby. Despite the sign saying not to, I opened the doors and picked up the bottle. There was something in it..."

"Something? Or someone?"

"Some*one*? That would be, well, as crazy as me talking to a ghost."

"Was the bottle made of pink glass? An odd hue?"

"Yes. I felt compelled to open the bottle. I even thought I heard the word *open*, like an order. Just as I was about to, that awful man shouted at me. I'm afraid I dropped the bottle, and it broke."

He was taking her in, his gaze moving from the top of her head down her body, then back to her face. "Thank God you broke it. I think I understand now. After that you walked into the bar and saw me, right?"

"Yes. Well, I'm glad *you* understand. Maybe you could, um, enlighten me. The one who's having bizarre experiences." And the bizarre urge to lean forward and kiss him.

Nate laughed, soft and low. He reached out and brushed a lock of her hair back with his fingers. But she couldn't feel it. "Perhaps I should show you something even more bizarre as a way to illustrate. Come with me." He reached for her hand, and she felt herself being tugged down a hallway, but again couldn't actually feel his touch. As she began to look down at their linked hands, he pulled her into a small bathroom with vintage wallpaper and antique sconces above

12

the sink. With a rush of what sounded like breath, he pushed at the light switch, and it came on. "Look at your reflection."

She gasped. Over her own reflection, Lorna could see the faint outline of that beautiful woman from the pictures, her dark hair tumbling down her shoulders. "Marina," she said on a breath. "But... how?"

"I've been looking for you, Marina. I knew you'd died too, but you weren't anywhere on the other side."

Lorna winced. "Maybe she went to..." She pointed down.

"Now that I'm over here, I understand that there is no eternal damnation. Only hell on Earth." His expression darkened. "That's what dying in that fire felt like. We're soulmates, and it didn't make sense that you weren't with me there. So I came back here. I sensed you were here, trapped somehow, but I couldn't find you. Then when you walked into the bar, I saw you. You, superimposed on Lorna."

"I am Lorna." But there was something odd going on. She was her and yet, she wasn't. The bizarreness of that made her sway, and he reached for her. But his hands went through her as he tried to steady her.

"Damn. I can touch Marina, but I can't touch you. It's difficult to touch a real surface." He took her in. "Are you all right?"

"Oh, just fine," she said on a sarcastic laugh. She gripped the white porcelain sink, staring at the hologram-like image in the mirror. "This is crazy. I don't even write stories like this. I didn't even give in on the paranormal trend when it became huge. How... how could this be?"

"I think I know. When you broke the bottle, you freed Marina's soul. She'd been trapped there. She and you have some kind of soul connection. Somehow she was able to reach out to you."

Lorna looked at him, with his seemingly flesh and blood body. "Now that I freed Marina, she can go on. And so can you."

"Yes, I suppose so."

"I kind of like her inside me, as weird as it feels. She gives me this spark of life. Sass."

He looked into her eyes, a mix of sadness and love in his. "You were a pistol. The spark of my life."

"Not me," Lorna corrected, though she felt a rush of answering love.

"Yes, you."

She had longed to hear words like that, the kind of devotion her heroes held for her heroines. Now she was privy to a love story in a much deeper dimension.

"Maybe if we hold hands, you can grab onto her spirit and go." With a last glance at the beautiful, ghostly image on her face, she walked back out to the living room. "Let's stand in the middle of the room." She instinctively reached out, and… "I feel you!" Not so much a physical touch but a vibration.

"Yes, me, too. Maybe because Marina is so strong in you right now. She and I are the same wavelength."

"I can feel her, too, in a different way. She was a good person. Kind and loving and compassionate." More than Lorna had been.

He smiled. "We shared something beyond definition. We are soulmates, not in the strictly romantic sense, but in a true soul way. You too are our soulmate. Yes, I feel it now. We're all part of the same soul group on the other side."

She wanted to know more, enchanted by the idea of belonging for the first time in her life. But there was something else she needed to know. "How did Marina's soul get trapped in a bottle?"

"Through a dark magic ceremony by a man obsessed with her. The man who killed us and set the fire to cover it up."

The door opened, and Gerard Tate stalked in. "What are you doing in here?" He looked around. "And who are you talking to?"

Nate glared at his former business partner. But his expression changed to fear as he shifted to her. "Make up some excuse and get out, Lorna."

Lorna. He'd used her name. Then his warning sank in—and what it meant. Gerard. He'd murdered Nate and Marina, then trapped her soul. If he could murder them, he'd have no problem killing her.

As she formed some flimsy excuse, Marina's words burst out of Lorna's mouth. "You murdering son of a bitch! You killed Nate because you wanted me. And when I caught you in the act, I fought you for the knife. You knew it was all over then. Your plan to be the consoling so-called friend wouldn't work now—nor would it have ever, just so you know. So you drove the knife into my stomach. While my life drained from me, you went to your grandmother's spell book. And you trapped me in that bottle!"

Gerard stood stock still for a moment. Finally, he uttered,

14

"*Marina?*"

Nate moved closer. "Run, Lorna!"

She started to run, aware that he couldn't see Nate. Gerard blocked her, knocking her to the bare wood floor. His hands clamped around her neck. "You freed her spirit, you dumb bi—"

Lorna rammed her knee into his balls, but he blocked her so the impact was lessened. He smacked her across the face, blacking out her vision for a second. He gripped her throat again and pressed hard. She writhed beneath him, but he'd pinned her with the full weight of his body. No… escape. She gasped for air, crumbling under the pain and lack of oxygen.

Nate pounded on Gerard's back, screaming, "No! Let her go! She's innocent!" The man flinched and looked over his right shoulder but didn't stop. He focused on her. "Die, cow."

Then Nate, with rage in his eyes, dove into Gerard. In her last conscious moments, she saw Nate superimposed over Gerard the way Marina had been on her. Gerard screamed, violently shaking his head. "Get out of me!"

Everything went dark…

She floated out of her body, but she saw nothing. Then a rush of life poured through her being. She opened her eyes, seeing the fresh plaster on the ceiling. Her hands went to her neck, and she hissed with pain. Her neck was bruised, and it hurt to draw breath.

But she *was* drawing breath.

She came to a sitting position and saw Gerard sprawled on the floor. She had to get away. But as she moved, his eyes opened.

No, no, no… panic roared through her.

But wait. Not anger in those dark eyes but wonder. And love.

"Nate?" she asked in a scratchy voice.

He struggled to sit up and cat-walked toward her. His hand cradled her cheek. "It's you." Then he smiled. "You're back."

"I think Lorna let me come in. I think… she was ready to go back home. To belong somewhere."

Nate gathered Marina in his arms. "Thank you, Lorna. I know we'll see you again."

Marina squeezed him tighter, hungry to feel him again. "She's with us too. I feel her inside me. Happy for the first time." She put her hand on her heart. "Someday we'll have a little girl, Nate."

He put his hand over hers. "And we'll name her Lorna."

2

THE LAST TRAIN OUT

Richard Devin

"Waiting." The word was unmistakable, even hidden within the chaos of the static. "Waiting."

Gus moved the Spirit Box in a slow methodical sweep. It was the first time he had attempted to use the apparatus and the location happened to be perfect: an isolated train platform, white tile walls that managed to shine despite the old, dim, dusty light falling from bulbs that Edison would recognize as coming straight from his New Jersey workshop.

Static poured from the Spirit Box. It was a noise that was both aggravating and intense, which tweaked his senses, making him hyper-aware.

"Waiting." The word broke the static, a moment of silence followed, then static.

Startled. He hadn't really expected the Spirit Box to work. *It did work! Didn't it?* Gus dismissed the question that slipped into his mind and forced himself to concentrate. He slowed the breath that was threatening to become heavy with fear... anticipation. He spoke aloud, "For what? What are you waiting for..." The static broke before he could finish the question.

"Train."

Gus took a step back as if to move away from the unseen presence. *Did it just answer me?* The voice had a feminine quality, slightly accented. The urge to run, to get out of the deepening shadows of the deserted train station nearly overcame him.

He fumbled, trying to maintain composure, pulled an EVP recorder from the pocket of his hoodie; switched it on. His intent was to record anything that came from the Spirit Box—words that he could hear, and anything that the ear could not pick up. The Electronic Voice Phenomenon recorder should, he hoped, had that ability.

"Waiting for what?" he asked, turning slowly, asked again. After a moment, he turned the Sprit Box off, silencing the unnerving white noise. Holding the EVP recorder at arm's length—as though it would somehow get him closer to the where the voice emanated—he asked again, "What are you waiting for?" He stood still, waiting, silent. A few minutes passed. He "rewound" the digital recorder, turned the volume dial to the high position, until it stopped. Then clicked the "play" button... and waited.

Dripping water.

A creak in the metal beams supporting the old train station.

The sound of air moving by.

Then...

A faint—as though it were miles away, and yet still recognizable—sound...

Cold steel wheels of a train screeching against the rails.

* * *

A week later, Gus was able to clear enough of the school work off his desk and make time to get back to the train station. He had played the recordings for several of the students in his class at UNR. It was definitely the sound of a train. He leaned against a red newspaper rack—that stood out among the row of black racks—just beyond the main entrance to the Reno train station. He had the Electronic Voice Phenomena recorder, the Spirit Box and a new gadget. It was a gift from a student in his UNR class on anthropology. He had never used it, thought it was hokey, but brought it along anyway. The gift was a "SUMS." It allegedly had the ability to detect and locate a moving spirit. The SUMS, along with the other paranormal contraptions, were laid out on top of the red rack, neatly arranged around a brownish blob that some bird had deposited. *Guess the bird didn't appreciate the headline that day.* Gus smiled at the thought.

He could feel the old depot building tremble as the wheels of the last train of the night braced the tracks, slowing the cars to a grinding, squealing stop.

Fifteen minutes later, Gus collected his tools, stuffing them into the various pockets of his vest, and headed inside the train station. The waiting room was empty. Long wooden benches lined up carefully below dimly lit chandeliers, and a coffered wooden ceiling, gave way to plastic airport-style seating, as Gus made his way to the lower platform.

Devoid of any decor, the lower platform was constructed in order to move the tracks below street level where the tracks had been for decades before. Contemporary traffic concerns and the flow of Reno traffic, forced the move. Concrete walls and walkways lined the "depressed" tracks… and that, they certainly were.

Gus contemplated starting the session with the Spirit Box, but the white noise that the box produced while "searching the airwaves" was so annoying and irritating, it put him on edge. Instead, he chose to start with the EVP recorder. Even though it wouldn't provide the same instantaneous communication as the Spirit Box, it was a less aggravating instrument to use.

Gus switched the EVP recorder on and slowly, as quietly as possible, walked around the platform.

Minutes later, after he had finished two treks around the platform, he rewound the recorder, hit play and listened.

Not a second into the playback… "I've been waiting."

Gus nearly dropped the recorder. Shaken and filled with excitement, he rewound the recorder, hit play; "I've been waiting." Rewound and hit play; "I've been waiting." He repeated the process several times afraid that the EVP would not remain.

It did.

He paused the device.

It was as clear as if the woman… *it was a woman. The same woman.* The realization that it was the same spirit he heard on the Spirit Box during the first session struck him. "Damn, this is real." He blurted the words out loud. "Damn!"

Rewound and hit play. He listened intently.

"I've been waiting."

There was a sadness that crept in around the edges of the words and a slight accent. The tape played on… a train.

Slowing. Squealing. Braking.

Then the unmistakable sound of steam escaping.

A blurred movement behind him caught his attention and caused the hair on his arms to stand.

He turned.

A woman stood in the corner of the platform. Hands wrapped around one another, she looked toward the tracks to an unseen train. Intense concern etched small lines around her eyes. Eyes that teared… with joy… with sadness?

Gus watched the hazy figure.

She never took her eyes off the phantom train. Never turned his way or acknowledged him.

She remained for a moment.

Then faded.

Gus fumbled with the EVP recorder hitting the playback button, nothing. He tried again. Nothing, not even static. Then he realized—he hadn't turned the recorder from playback to record. "Damn it!" He gritted his teeth against the anger roiling up.

"Waiting."

He spun around.

The voice was so close. The words so clear.

No one stood beside him. He turned and looked on the other side of the platform. He was alone.

A breeze touched his arm.

He spun, took several steps back and felt his balance give way as his foot reached the edge of the concrete platform.

Too late. He fought to right himself, swinging his arms to correct his balance. He was already leaning too far over the edge. Weight and moment took control. He fell. The EVP recorder slipped from his hands as he instinctively reached out to break the fall. One hand landed on the track—oddly he took in the sensation of the cold steel on his flesh before his head followed—hitting that same cold steel…

His vision blurred, cleared slightly, blurred again. He blinked, strained to focus… then gave in to the swirling cloud of confusion. His eyes closed, and he allowed the blackness to envelop him.

* * *

"Sir? Sir?" The voice was muffled. "Do you know where you

are?" The gruff voice asked more loudly than before. "Sir, do you understand me?"

Gus opened his eyes to a smeared vision of a face with a three-day beard. "That's good, open your eyes," the man instructed. "Can you see me?"

He couldn't. He fought to keep his eyes open. Fought to clear his vision. Fought the blackness that beckoned... and won.

* * *

A hand caressed his face and pushed the hair back from his forehead. It was in that moment between sleep and wake, light and darkness. He remained still comforted by the soft stroking of his hair. After a moment, he pulled himself from slumber. Opening his eyes. Slowly his vision began to clear.

* * *

Her eyes overflowed with tears. Her smile lingered for a brief moment, before giving way to concern. She brushed his face with the back of her hand, then pulled him close to her body, wrapping her arms tightly around him.

People pushed by; she didn't let go; she didn't care. They could step around. She breathed in the musty, musky scent of his uniform.

Behind them, the unmistakable sound of steam escaping as the train strained to pull from the station. Metal against metal pushed on by steam to roll forward.

"Waiting," She spoke, still wrapped as tightly against him as she could possibly be. "Waiting. The waiting is over." She pushed herself back from him, looked into his dark—nearly black eyes. "Our waiting is over. Agustino." She reached up and caressed his face with her hand. "You're home." She leaned in and kissed him gently on the forehead.

* * *

He responded, taking her into his arms, pressing his body to hers. His lips sought out hers and seared into them with a longing he had not known existed. He lost control. A long aching void erupted. He held on to her, afraid to let her go.

She laughed, tossing her head back, then placed a hand against his chest holding him back. "Agustino, we are in public." She laughed again, the sly smile that spread across her face betrayed her true thoughts.

"I don't care," he wrapped his arms tightly around her waist, pulling into him. He kissed her.

* * *

She relented, giving into to him. Her lips responded to his; her arms wrapped around his shoulders and clenched him with all the might she had. She could feel the heat of his body penetrating through her day dress.

She had worn the dress the last time she had held him. The last time she had seen him. It was the day he stepped onto the train.

Images of those last moments together, of him, flashed into her thoughts, like a series of photos from a Vest Pocket Kodak: He smiled back at her, stepped onto the train. Nodded to her. Smiled again—a smile that watery eyes betrayed. Turned, and walked out of sight.

He was heading to Camp Lewis in Washington State to join up with the 91st. The "Wild West" division, she laughed when he told her that. Wild West it was. His ability to break and train horses was in high demand, so like many others from Las Vegas, Reno and Virginia City, he met President's Wilson's call and had enlisted.

That was the spring of 1917.

In November of 1918 the war came to end.

And Rose's vigil began.

* * *

"Rose?" Gus whispered her name as though he was suddenly remembering it. "Rose?"

She looked into his eyes. "Of course it's me."

"You waited." His eyes glistened with tears. "You waited for me."

"Every day. Every day, Agustino." She grasped his hands in an unconscious attempt to keep him from leaving again. "Every day since November 11, the day that terrible war ended. I knew you would come back to me, Gus. I never gave up." She brushed away the tears that slid from her eyes. "I've come to the station and waited for you, every day." She couldn't contain the tears any longer. They burst forth. She sobbed with both overwhelming joy and desperate relief. "The train would come. But you wouldn't be on it. Every day the train would come, and I would wait. Then the train would leave… leaving me alone. Every day the same." Her slight accent accentuated the words. "I never gave up Gus, I never gave up. I knew you would come back to me."

"I'll never leave you again Rose, I promise. I will never…" His words slurred as his eyes involuntarily closed and he was pulled back into the darkness.

* * *

The sound was jarring. It tore at his thoughts, and like the call of a piper, beckoned him to follow. Cold swept over him. Fingers and toes numb.

"Twenty-seven, twenty-eight, twenty-nine, and breathe." The voice was distant, faint, gruff.

Air forced its way into his lungs. He choked it back, then another blast hit him hard. One, two, three… His chest felt like it was going to collapse. Pressure applied, released, applied again. Pain followed each thrust. His ribs ached. He wanted to push the pain away, and begged his arms to move. They remained still, at his side, flopping with the each of the thrusts.

"Twenty-seven, twenty-eight, twenty-nine and breathe."

Again, air made its way forcefully into his lungs.

"Come on, man, you're going to make it."

Gus willed his body to resist. He turned his mind's eye from the blackness, pain and confusion, to the light.

A voice filled with desperation, called to him.

"Waiting."

He tried to respond, but his own voice was silenced, as another burst of air filled his lungs.

"Twenty-eight, twenty-nine, breathe."

His body relented, responded to pressure… choking, followed by fits of coughing, and a deep burning in his lungs as sensations returned.

The pounding on his chest ceased.

He lay still. Clouded mind clearing.

Gus open his eyes slightly.

A sweating, exhausted face that was distantly recognizable came into focus.

"You're doing great, buddy." The EMT wiped at his forehead with his shirtsleeve. "Hang in there."

A fit of coughs struck him. Raw pain filled his throat and lungs with every breath. He teetered on the edge of consciousness. Voices all around him echoing blurred words, that swirled in his mind— whirlwind of confusion. He gagged as another fit of coughs struck him. He felt his body forcefully being pulled to his side.

And at the edge of his vision… saw her.

In the corner of the station platform, Rose stood, hands wrapped around one another. A tear slowly slid down the side of her face.

She looked directly at him. Her cocked to one side. A slow smile moved across her face. She nodded. And began to fade.

"No!" Gus found his voice. "No Rose. No."

"It's okay buddy, you're going to be ok." The EMT's words had a reassuring quality to them. "We're going to get you to the hospital. You're going to be ok."

Gus reached forward, his open hand grasping at the slowly fading, distant image. "Rose. Rose." His voice grew weak, he strained to speak. "Rose…"

"I'll be waiting." Rose said and reached in his direction. "Always," she faded becoming like the edge of fog.

Gus's body heaved. He twisted, turned and fell onto his back. Spasms wracked him. His legs arched up and kicked out. He could feel the EMT's hands pushing on his arms, legs, and chest trying to hold him down. Muffled shouts, voices of concern accompanied the EMT's struggles.

Gus fought. He fought back as hard as the energy in him would allow, pushing against the EMT's arms, grasping them in a desperate attempt.

Gus fought with the last bit of strength he had.

He fought… not to stay.

But to go.

"Rose." He reached for her. His voice wheezed as he took his last breath, and felt her hand take his. And let the light overtake him.

3

OUTLAW GHOST

Kat Martin

Chapter One

Sweet Springs, Texas

A harsh wind pulled at the branches outside the window. The howl of a coyote echoed mournfully from the hills overlooking the property at the edge of town. Beneath the old-fashioned quilt on the antique iron bed, Callie Sutton listened to a different sound, this one coming from inside the old Victorian house.

It was an eerie sound, disturbing, a strangely human sound. As if someone walked through the silent rooms then climbed the stairs. As if someone opened the door and came into her room. As if he stood at the foot of her bed.

Since the door was firmly closed and locked, it was impossible, yet the feeling of being watched would not go away.

The tempo of her heart increased, and her nerves stretched taut as Callie searched the darkness but found no one there. She told herself it was all in her mind, nothing more than the normal creaks and groans of a house this old. The Victorian home she had inherited from a distant aunt had been empty and in disrepair for more than thirty years.

But the moment she had seen the charming turret in front and wrap-around porch, the lovely built-in bookcases, molded ceilings and ornate woodwork, she had fallen in love with the place.

The renovations she'd had done before she moved in were mostly finished, the kitchen and baths remodeled, the hardwood floors refinished, the fireplace repaired and a fire crackling in the hearth in the evenings.

The work that remained was mostly superficial and of course she had a ton of decorating to do. Callie was looking forward to that. Or at least she had been until the ghostly sounds in the house at night continued to grow more pronounced.

Awake now, Callie stared up at the ceiling, her ears straining for any indication of a threat, but the house had fallen silent. Eventually, her heartbeat returned to normal and her body relaxed.

She yawned, sleepy from a long day at the clinic and putting up wallpaper in the kitchen when she got home after work.

As a veterinarian technician, she had been hired by the county vet, Dr. Reynolds, who was badly in need of help. Callie worked mostly with small animals, while Doc Reynolds specialized in large animals, a necessity in a ranching community like the tiny Texas town of Sweet Springs.

Since the clinic at the end of Main Street was always busy, Callie would be facing another hectic day tomorrow. She needed to get some sleep. She yawned again and her eyes drifted closed as an odd sense of peace stole over her. It had happened before and perhaps that was the reason she wasn't more afraid.

She didn't believe in ghosts. On the other hand, if there were such a thing, this one seemed strangely protective. A smile touched her lips as she drifted deeper into sleep and Callie started to dream.

He was tall, in snug dark pants, a full-sleeved white linen shirt, and tall black boots. He wore a black flat-brimmed hat, and a gun belt hung from his lean hips, the pistol strapped to a muscled thigh. She tried to see his face beneath the brim of the hat but caught just the hint of a hard jaw covered by several days' growth of dark beard.

He stood at the foot of the bed as if he watched over her. He looked like an outlaw, she thought in some corner of her mind, a gunslinger right out of the Wild West. She should have been frightened but she wasn't afraid. Instead she felt safe, protected.

She settled into an even deeper sleep and didn't wake up until morning, the dream no more than a hazy memory.

Callie showered and dressed in jeans and a lightweight sweater just warm enough for the end-of-October weather, then headed downstairs for coffee and toast before she drove to work.

She loved her newly remodeled country kitchen. She'd almost had the servant's stairs removed but they were part of the original structure, so she had left them. Turned out they were handy and added a certain charm. She'd found an antique oak table and topped it with pretty yellow placemats that matched the walls, making the big kitchen feel cozy.

Callie glanced at the table, an uneasy feeling creeping through her. At the sight of the single red rose lying on top, her insides tightened. Someone had been inside the house!

Her hands shook as she pulled the phone out of her pocket and dialed 9-1-1. Dear God, was the intruder still somewhere inside? Her gaze shot to the back door, saw that the lock had been pried open, and a chill rolled down her spine.

She thought of the eerie sounds in the house last night and how she had felt safe and protected.

Clearly she wasn't as safe as she thought.

Chapter Two

"Sweet Springs Sheriff's Office," a woman's voice answered. "Millie speaking, what's your emergency?"

"Someone broke into my house last night. They left a rose on my kitchen table while I was asleep upstairs."

"A rose, huh? Old boyfriend, maybe?" Clearly a town the size of Sweet Springs didn't have a lot of crime.

"I don't have any old boyfriends," Callie said. "I just moved here. I-I'm afraid he might still be in the house."

Millie's voice sobered. "What's your address?"

Callie gave her the property address on Pecan Lane. "It's the old Victorian at the edge of town."

"Stay on the line. I'm calling Sheriff Trask. He isn't that far away."

Callie's stomach churned for the entire five minutes that passed before she heard the crunch of gravel and the engine of a vehicle pulling up in front. Through the dining room window, she saw a white, extended cab pickup, the word SHERIFF in big blue letters on the door.

The sheriff got out, a tall man in a dark brown uniform, pants and a light beige short-sleeved shirt, a badge pinned to the front. He wore a beige cowboy hat and a pistol holstered on the belt at his waist.

"He's here," Callie said to Millie with relief. The call ended, and she hurried to the front door to let him in.

"Callie Sutton?" the sheriff asked, looking down at her from beneath the brim of his hat. He had the bluest eyes Callie had ever seen.

"That's me. Please come in."

"Sheriff Brendan Trask. Let me take a look around then we'll talk."

"Thank you. I don't think he's still here, but I don't know for sure."

He nodded and started moving silently through the house. She noticed he unsnapped the flap on his holster, and the chill returned.

Callie was five-foot-three, the sheriff at least a foot taller. He was swarthy and with his strong jaw and incredible blue eyes, he was handsome. A pair of powerful biceps stretched the sleeves of his uniform shirt. His shoulders were wide, his waist and hips narrow.

If he wasn't married, he was probably the most eligible bachelor in Sweet Springs County.

He returned a few minutes later. "Nobody here. Looks like he came in through the back door."

"I guess I should have bought a better lock."

"Rob Solomon over at the hardware store can sell you something reliable. He can put it on for you, too."

"Okay, thanks."

"Millie mentioned the rose. You found it on the kitchen table?"

"Yes. I haven't touched anything." She glanced toward the kitchen. "I suppose it could be kids or someone's idea of a joke. If it is, it isn't funny."

"Breaking and entering is never a joke, Ms. Sutton."

They walked together into the kitchen and he took a second look around, focused his attention on the rose. "You didn't hear anything?"

How to answer. She heard the same noises she'd been hearing every night, the sound of a man's boots on the stairs and someone walking into her bedroom. But she couldn't tell the sheriff there might be a ghost in the house.

It was ridiculous. She didn't even believe in ghosts.

"I didn't hear anything that sounded like a door being forced open or anyone moving around in the kitchen. *Just someone upstairs in my room.* But she didn't think a ghost could force open a door or carry a rose into the kitchen.

"I want to dust the door for prints. I'll be right back." The sheriff disappeared outside and returned with what she assumed was a fingerprint kit.

He set his hat aside as he dusted the door and the table, and she admired his thick, slightly too long, dark brown hair. He bagged the rose as evidence and asked her a few more questions, then she walked him to the door.

"Be sure and take care of that lock," he said.

"I'll call Rob Solomon right away."

He nodded, glanced around the living room. "You did a nice job restoring the place. Looks like it must have more than a hundred years ago, only better."

She smiled at the compliment. "Thank you." Not many people had been over for a visit since she'd moved in, just her best friend, Lanni Bridges, who'd come down from San Antonio, and one of the girls who worked part time for Dr. Reynolds.

The sheriff pulled open the front door. "Like you said, it's probably just kids, but you don't want to take any chances." Those amazing blue eyes fixed on her face. "I'll give you my cell phone number. I don't live far away. If you hear something, call me."

She punched his number into her phone. As the sheriff put his hat back on and settled the brim low across his forehead, Callie felt a warm tug in the pit of her stomach.

She blinked in surprise. She hadn't felt the least attraction to a man since she and Adam had split up almost a year ago.

"I'll keep you posted on what I find out," Sheriff Trask said.

Callie watched him walk away and tried not to think he looked nearly as good from the back as the front. She hadn't noticed a wedding ring, but that didn't mean he wasn't married or seriously involved with someone. A man like that had his choice of women.

Not that it really mattered. She was too busy getting settled at the clinic to think about a man.

Well, other than the ghost upstairs.

Chapter Three

After a hard day at the animal clinic that included a battle with a wily Siamese cat named Hugo armed with the sharpest claws Callie ever had seen. She prayed for an uneventful evening. Besides working late to help the doctor sew up a car-chasing dog hit by a pickup, she had worried about her intruder all day.

The house was quiet when she got home, no sign of anything out of place. She zapped a frozen lasagna dinner in the newly installed microwave, ate, and went straight up to bed. She drifted off more easily than she had expected and settled into a deep slumber.

She wasn't sure when she started to dream, only that the tall outlaw cowboy was back in her room, and this time he was in her bed.

He was leaning over her, kissing the side of her neck, his big hands lightly caressing her breasts through her thin, white nylon nightgown. She moaned as he trailed kisses along her throat and over her cheek, and soft male lips settled on her mouth.

Warmth spread through her, slid into her core. *It's a dream*, she told herself as a memory of last night's dream returned. *Why not enjoy it?*

Parting her lips, she opened to invite her dream lover in and the kiss turned hot and deep. A hard chest pressed against her breasts and big calloused hands roamed over her body.

It had been so long since anyone had touched her that way, so long since she had actually felt this kind of desire.

The dream shifted a little and he was naked, his body hard and muscled over hers. She could feel his heavy arousal nestled between her legs—for a dream, it was incredibly real.

She allowed the fantasy to continue, her body responding to the skillful touches of the outlaw's hands and the saturating pleasure of his mouth moving hotly over hers.

When a noise downstairs penetrated her senses, threatening to disturb the dream, irritation trickled through her. Damn, she didn't want the dream to end. With a sigh of resignation, Callie stirred awake and opened her eyes, expecting to be looking at the ceiling above the bed.

Instead, she stared into the bluest eyes she had ever seen. Callie screamed.

Chapter Four

In an instant, the man was gone, vanished like the ghostly vision he had been.

Her heart was racing, her body still flushed with heat. Callie tried to tell herself the face of the outlaw she had seen was just part of the dream, that she hadn't awoken and seen a blue-eyed man in bed with her who looked almost exactly like the handsome county sheriff.

It was the *almost* that was the problem. The outlaw had a scar along the bottom of his jaw that the sheriff did not have.

The noise came again, pulling her back from the fantasy, the sound of glass shattering downstairs—someone breaking the window in the kitchen. Fresh fear assailed her. The ghost was gone but what about the man who had broken into her house last night?

She grabbed her phone off the nightstand and hit the sheriff's contact number.

"Trask," he said, his voice crystal clear, as if he'd instantly come awake.

"Sheriff, it's...it's Callie Sutton. He's... he's in the house. He broke out a window. Oh, God... he's... coming up the stairs."

"On my way. Lock yourself in the bathroom, Callie. Stay there till I tell you to come out. I'll keep the line open, but the call may drop. I'll be there as fast as I can."

She heard fabric rustling as Trask pulled on his clothes. Callie grabbed her white terry robe and hurriedly shrugged it on.

As she turned toward the bathroom, she heard sounds outside the bedroom door. A struggle, some kind of fight going on, a foul curse, then the heavy thud of something crashing down the stairs.

Oh, dear God. "Sheriff? Sheriff Trask are you there?"

But as he had warned, the call had dropped, and the line was dead. *He's on his way,* she reminded herself. *All I have to do is survive until he gets here.*

Her gaze shot to the bedroom door. Rob Solomon had installed a new lock on the kitchen door downstairs, but the lock on the bedroom door was old and hadn't been replaced. She should barricade herself in the bathroom as Sheriff Trask had told her, but the lock was no better in there, and she didn't like the idea of being trapped inside.

Callie listened. The only sound was the fierce beating of her heart. Instead of the usual creaks and groans, the house was eerily silent. Too silent, she thought, a shiver running over her skin.

Headlights flashed into the bedroom. She hurried to the window and saw Sheriff Trask's pickup pull up in front of the house. *Thank you, God.*

Her cell phone rang. She answered with unsteady hands.

"Callie, are you all right?"

"I think he's gone. Just in case, I'll come down the back stairs and let you in through the kitchen."

"Be careful," Trask said.

Callie grabbed the flashlight she kept beside the bed, unlocked the bedroom door, and peered into the hall. Seeing nothing, she quietly headed for the servants' stairs leading down to the kitchen. As she passed the round oak table, she shined a light on top and there it was–another long-stemmed red rose.

Fear quickened her footsteps. She unlocked the newly installed deadbolt, the sheriff strode into the kitchen, and relief poured through her.

"Stay here." His gun was in his hand as he made his way out of the kitchen and began to search the house.

She couldn't help noticing the lack of a scar beneath his hard jaw.

Chapter Five

Brendan moved silently though the house, quietly checking each room. *First floor clear.* He headed for the staircase, shined his light in that direction and stopped cold in his tracks.

Death had an aura about it. The bald, muscular man sprawled on the stairs with his mouth gaping open, sightless eyes staring up at the ceiling, reeked of it.

Brendan knelt to check for a pulse, but there was really no need. He stepped back and took a moment to study the scene. From the angle of the man's neck and the way the body had landed, it didn't look like the guy could have accidentally fallen down the stairs.

Brendan's gaze shot to the landing at the top. If it wasn't an accident, who had killed him? Was the perp still in the house? Brendan made a room-by-room search but found no sign of an intruder. He returned to the crime scene and phoned the coroner, a local physician named Elias Halpern, rousing him from sleep.

Brendan looked back at the dead man on the stairs. The guy was big and strong. Had the pretty little brunette in the kitchen somehow managed to overpower him? It didn't seem likely. Even if by some miracle she had killed him, he was trespassing in her house. The lady would have been justified, at least as far as Brendan was concerned. Still, she could be in for a lot of trouble and legal expense.

Brendan thought about her as he returned to the kitchen. He had run a check on her after the first call she'd made. Callie Marie Sutton was twenty-seven, just five years younger than he was, originally from San Antonio. With her big brown eyes, long dark brown curls, and dynamite figure, he hadn't been able to get her out of his mind since the first time he had seen her.

He and Deb Younger were no longer dating. If Callie gave any indication she was interested, Brendan planned to ask her out.

He just hoped like hell she wasn't a killer.

<u>Chapter Six</u>

Awaiting the sheriff's return, which seemed to take forever, Callie tightened the sash on her robe and wished she'd had time to put on some clothes. Finally, Trask walked back into the kitchen, his features grim.

His glance strayed to the table and he noticed the long-stemmed red rose.

"It was him," she said, her pulse hammering again.

"Looks like." He fixed her with a stare. "But you don't need to worry about him anymore."

"You caught him?"

"Your admirer is lying at the bottom of the staircase. He's dead."

Callie gripped the back of a kitchen chair. "He... he fell down the stairs?"

"No, Callie. He was pushed."

The coroner arrived, a local physician who said his name was Elias Halpern. While Dr. Halpern examined the body, Callie sat in the kitchen drinking coffee, doing her best not to think of the dead man in the other room and answer the sheriff's questions.

"So you heard noises on the stairs but you didn't go outside your bedroom to see what was going on?"

"I told you, I was waiting for you to get here." She frowned. "In a roundabout way, that's the third time you've asked me the same question. You don't think *I'm* the one who pushed that man down the stairs?"

Before Sheriff Trask had time to answer, Dr. Halpern walked in, an older man with thinning gray hair and glasses. "It wasn't Ms. Sutton," he said. "Bruising on the neck indicates a big man's hands, someone strong and extremely fit. The struggle didn't last long, then one good shove and it was over. This little gal ain't big enough nor strong enough to do the job."

Trask looked relieved. "Looks like you're in the clear, Ms. Sutton."

"I wasn't really worried since I knew I didn't kill him."

Trask's sexy mouth edged up and she felt a slide of heat. It was crazy considering the circumstances.

His smile faded. "This is a crime scene. Is there somewhere you can stay for a day, maybe two?"

"I just moved here. I don't know many people. The Westerner Motel will have to do."

He nodded. "Pack what you need and I'll follow you over there. Use the back stairs so you don't disturb anything."

"All right. So… who do you think killed him?"

"We'll no more in a couple of days."

Callie hoped so. But as she climbed the backstairs to her room, a strange thought occurred. Was it possible for a ghost to kill?

While the sheriff spent the next few days searching for a killer, Callie went to work searching the past for the man she thought of as her protector.

<u>Chapter Seven</u>

After the murder–as the coroner had labeled it–her boss at the clinic, Dr. Reynolds, had insisted she take the next day off. Callie used the time to begin her search, starting at the local library.

She wanted to know the history of the house, who built it, who had lived there, who might have had a reason to stay in the house long after he was dead.

It was insane. No way was the man in her dreams a ghost. On the other hand, the intimate kiss they'd shared in her bedroom seemed far more real than any dream.

Fortunately, the task she had set for herself proved easier than she had imagined. The old Victorian was a landmark in the community. Barb Dawson, the local librarian, a silver-haired lady in her seventies, knew all about it.

"I love history," Barb said. "It's one of the reasons I wanted to be a librarian. Since my family has lived in the county for three generations, I know all about Sweet Springs."

"My aunt, Mary Sutton, owned the house before she died and left it to me. Can you tell me who owned it before my aunt?"

Barb walked over to a big leather-bound book, set it on the library table, and opened it. She shoved her half glasses up on her nose.

She ran a finger down the list of names. "Otto Lansing. Now I remember. Lansing built the house in the eighteen sixties as an anniversary gift. He and his wife lived there a few years then sold the place to the Trask family. They were some of Sweet Springs original settlers."

Callie's head came up. "Sheriff Trask's family?"

"That's right. He's a descendant, named after a great-great-great grandfather. The first Brendan Trask lived here with his wife Priscilla before they moved out to the ranch. Ranch stayed in the family. Land belongs to the sheriff now, though he doesn't do much ranching these days."

Callie's mind was spinning, running through possibilities, all of which connected the blue-eyed outlaw in her dreams to the equally blue-eyed Sweet Springs sheriff.

"The Trasks were very successful ranchers," Barb continued. "When they moved out of the house, they rented the place instead of selling it. Years later, when Priscilla began to have medical problems, they moved back in. She was in her eighties by then. She died peacefully in her sleep, and her husband sold the house. He died a few months later. A real love story, it was. Kind of a romantic legend."

"You wouldn't have any sort of photo of the original Brendan Trask?"

"The library doesn't but the sheriff has all kinds of family memorabilia."

And since Trask had called to say he needed to speak to her in regard to the case, she would have a chance to ask him about it.

Barb returned her attention to the book and went down the list of owners through the years, using county clerk records, but Callie had the information she needed, at least for now.

"The house is more than a hundred fifty years old," Callie said, approaching the subject carefully. "Anybody ever say anything about ghosts?"

Barb shook her head. "Nope, not that I ever heard. Kids used to make up stuff to try to scare each other, but none of the owners ever said anything like that. At least nothing that was ever passed down."

Callie wasn't sure if that was good news or bad. "Thanks, Barb. You've been a great help."

"No problem. Always fun to talk history."

From the library, Callie drove to the Sheriff's office on Main Street at the opposite end of town. With it's false-front brick buildings and slant parking in front of the stores, Sweet Springs had an appealing, old-fashioned charm. Or at least Callie thought so.

The sheriff's white pickup sat in front of the office when Callie walked in, ringing the bell over the door.

"May I help you?" a large woman behind the counter asked, MILLIE, read the sign on her desk.

"I'm looking for Sheriff Trask. I talked to you the other night. Thanks for your help, by the way."

"You must be Callie Sutton. I'm glad you're okay. Welcome to Sweet Springs."

Callie looked up as the sheriff walked out of his office. He smiled when he saw her and she felt a little kick. There was something about a man uniform, or so it was said. Plus this man was just flat-out hot.

"I'm glad you stopped by, Callie," he said. "I was on my way out to get something to eat. You got time to join me?"

"I'm off today. I could use something myself."

The sheriff seemed pleased. She figured he probably just wanted to discuss the case, but she couldn't help hoping it was more.

At the Sweet Springs Café, they sat down in a red vinyl booth across from each other and both ordered burgers and fries.

"So how is the case coming along?" Callie asked as the waitress brought their food. "Do you have any leads?"

Trask swallowed the bite of burger he had taken and set the rest back down on his plate. "On the killer? No. No DNA, no fingerprints. Nothing left at the crime scene. The guy did a spectacular job of cleaning up. Must have been a pro."

Or he wasn't really a guy, or at least not the living, breathing kind.

"We IDed the man who broke into your house. His name's Raymond Whitley. He's wanted for serial rape."

The French fry she had just picked up dropped from her suddenly nerveless fingers. "Oh, my God."

"Whitley's signature was a single red rose. He broke into his victim's home and left a rose while she was sleeping. Then he returned on a different night to attack her. He was brutal, liked to inflict pain. Four women that we know of—all ended up in the hospital."

Callie swallowed, no longer hungry.

"His last victim was in a small town outside Shreveport, Louisiana. No reason to think he'd show up here. You're a very lucky woman, Callie."

"Yes...yes, I am." But maybe it wasn't luck. Maybe someone had saved her. Someone who looked a lot like Sheriff Trask. "I was wondering...I've been researching the history of the house. Barb Dawson told me it once belonged to your family. Would you happen to have any information on the Trask family who lived there?"

The sheriff smiled, a flash of white against his swarthy skin. "I've got a ton of old stuff out at the ranch. I'm not a great cook, but I'm a kick-ass barbeque griller. I could fix you dinner and show you what I've got."

"No wife or kids?"

"Nope. Never found the right woman."

She toyed with another fry. "Barb told me about Brendan and Priscilla. I guess you're waiting for that kind of romance."

The look in those intense blue eyes softened on her face. "Yeah, I guess I am."

Callie couldn't tear her gaze away. "I'd love to come out for supper," she said softly.

Trask's eyes remained on her face. "How about tonight?"

"What time?"

"Gets dark early. I could pick you up around six. It's not that far to the ranch house."

Chapter Eight

Brendan was right. It wasn't that far. The original ranch house was gone, he told her as they drove along the two-lane road. She couldn't see much through the darkness, but she knew the terrain was rugged in places, lots of trees and the river not far away. The house had been built by his parents, Brendan said, who had wanted to be closer to town. He'd moved back in a few years ago, when his dad and mom retired to Florida, a long-time dream.

He pulled up to a two-story brick house with upstairs dormer windows and a long-covered porch out front. "Welcome to my humble abode." Brendan went around and helped her down from his truck then walked her to the door.

"I haven't changed much since I moved in," he said as they stepped into the entry. "I'll get around to it eventually."

Callie glanced at the comfortable living room furniture, the antique buffet, the handmade doilies. "I like it. It has a very warm feeling."

"It's homey, I guess."

"Nothing wrong with that."

They went into the kitchen and Brendan poured her a glass of white wine. He grabbed a beer for himself then started making supper.

As eager as she was to see the information Brendan might have on his family, she decided to relax and enjoy herself. She was out with a gorgeous man and she hadn't done anything but work since she had moved to Sweet Springs.

She smiled as she watched him work. Brendan was a serious griller. While Callie made a salad and put a couple of potatoes in to bake, the sheriff used his big stainless barbeque to perfectly cook two medium rare steaks.

It was a delicious meal and Brendan was a good conversationalist, asking questions about her job and telling stories about his work as county sheriff.

From the moment she had met him, she'd felt a deep pull of attraction, not just because of his good looks and hard muscled body, but because he was smart, and she felt that she could trust him.

The attraction seemed to be mutual, reflected in those amazing blue eyes. There was heat there, plenty of it. Like the blue tip of a flame.

When the meal was over, she helped him clear the dishes, then he led her into the living where an overstuffed burgundy sofa and chairs sat in front of a manteled brick fireplace. Photos dominated the wall above an antique mahogany buffet.

"You wanted to know about my family. I've got old letters, photo albums, all kinds of stuff. The photos are my favorite."

Callie walked over for a closer look, an odd sensation prickling her skin. "Some of these pictures are really old."

He nodded. "The daguerreotypes date back to the eighteen sixties."

She studied the early tin-types. Two, in particular, caught her eye, a man and a woman in oval mahogany frames facing each other. Her pulse quickened. "It's them, isn't it? Those two photos. Brendan and Priscilla."

He nodded. "Silla, he called her. He would have been in his late thirties, early forties at the time the picture was made." He turned toward her. "There're a lot of photos up there. How did you know which ones they were?"

She toyed with a pretty lace doily on the sideboard. "If I tell you, you'll think I'm crazy." She gazed up at him. "I don't want that to happen. I really like you, Brendan."

He smiled. God, she loved the way he smiled, like it was always close, ready to surface at the first opportunity.

"I really like you, too, Callie." One of his big hands settled at her waist and he drew her closer, until they were touching full length. He framed her face between his palm and Callie closed her eyes as he tipped her head back and settled his mouth over hers. Softly at first, then deeper, their lips melding, fitting perfectly together.

A little whimper escaped at the rush of heat that burned through her and her arms slid up around his neck. She could feel the muscles moving beneath his shirt as Brendan deepened the kiss, which went on and on, long, hot, and hungry, thoroughly arousing.

The ghostly Trask had nothing on the living, breathing version standing right in front of her. When the kiss finally ended, Callie swayed toward him, and Brendan steadied her.

He ran a finger along her cheek. "I had a feeling it was going to be like that."

Callie looked up at him. "So did I." But then she'd had a sneak preview.

Brendan's gaze returned to the pictures on the wall and Callie's gaze followed. "You thought it was the outlaw Trask because he looks like me?" he asked.

Outlaw. Shock rolled through her. "Your great-great-great grandfather was an outlaw?"

"For a while he was. He was pardoned. Something about helping catch a bunch of smugglers down in Natchez. They wrote a book about him, one of those pulp fiction westerns that made him more of a hero than he probably was. It's called *Natchez Flame.*"

"I'd love to read it sometime."

Brendan studied the photos, including one taken with the couple and their kids years later. "You know, you look a lot like Priscilla."

She'd noticed that, too. "I've done some family genealogy. I don't think we're related, but looking at her picture, I can certainly see the resemblance. It's uncanny how much I look like her." She studied the face of the woman with big dark eyes and thick dark hair. Same chin, same nose, same mouth. "Maybe that explains it."

"Explains what?"

She turned and looked up at him, into those amazing blue eyes. "The reason he came back to the house. Maybe he thinks I'm Silla."

"Wait a minute—"

"I know, I know. But he's been coming into my bedroom at night. At first I thought I was dreaming, but one night... one night he kissed me, and I opened my eyes and I saw him. He was dressed like an outlaw or a gunslinger. He looked just like you, Brendan, except for the scar below his jaw."

"Whoa. You think the ghost of my great-great-great grandfather is in your house?"

She managed to nod. "He's young, though. Somewhere around your age."

"Sorry. I don't believe in ghosts."

"Neither do I. At least I never did. You know what's even crazier? I think he protected me the night Raymond Whitley broke into the house to rape me. I think Brendan killed him."

Chapter Nine

She hadn't seen Brendan for the last three days. She'd said she had seen a ghost. He thought she was crazy. No way would he ever call her again. It bothered her more than it should have, considering

39

how little time they'd spent together.

It was probably that amazing kiss. She couldn't remember a kiss affecting her so strongly, turning her knees to jelly and setting her body on fire. She'd wanted to tear off his clothes and drag him into the bedroom. She'd wanted to make love with him all night long and start again in the morning.

It wasn't like her. She hadn't thought about sex for nearly a year, not since she had ended things with Adam. Now Brendan was gone and there was no way he was coming back. It made her heart hurt a little.

She was working at the clinic when her cell phone rang, just finished stitching up a little white schnauzer that had cuts its paw on a barbed wire fence.

"I'll finish up," Dr. Reynolds said. He was mid-forties, a little too thin and a really nice guy. "Go ahead and take the call."

Callie hurried over and picked up the phone. "This is Callie."

"It's Brendan. Have you got a minute?"

Her stomach clenched. For him, she had all the time in the world. "I'm not busy at the moment." She walked into the back room for a little privacy, the phone pressed against her ear.

"I can't stop thinking about you, Callie. I really want to see you."

A warm feeling spread through her. She'd begun to accept that she wouldn't be seeing him again. "I'd like that, too."

"Good. That's great. Has the... ahh... ghost been back?"

Her fingers tightened around the phone. She didn't want to talk about ghosts. She didn't to ruin things again. "No, not since... not since the night of the murder."

"I'm glad to hear it," he said firmly. Something in his voice. Impossible as it seemed, it sounded a lot like jealousy.

"I know someone who... ahh... thinks she can help," he said. "Any chance the two of us could come over tonight?"

He wanted to see her. He wanted to help her. He wanted to come over to the house. The warm feelings expanded. "Tonight would work."

"Say eight o'clock?"

"All right. I'll see you then." She ended the call but still held onto the phone. Brendan was coming over. She glanced at the clock. It was almost six. If nothing last-minute came up, she could go home and figure out what to wear. She wanted to look good for him.

She just hoped all this talk about ghosts wasn't going to send him running again.

Chapter Ten

Brendan stood on her doorstep at exactly eight p.m. "Miss Aggie, this is Callie Sutton. Callie, I'd like you to meet Agatha Hennessey. Everyone calls her Miss Aggie."

Callie smiled. "It's nice to meet you, Miss Aggie."

"Miss Aggie's from over in Jasper County." His gaze went to the woman beside him. She was huge. Not tall, but square, built like a box. She must have weighed three hundred pounds. "Miss Aggie is a seer. My mom used to visit her for... ahh... advice."

Callie inwardly smiled. The sheriff must have had an interesting family.

"I appreciate your trying to help, Miss Aggie. Please come in." Callie stepped back to welcome her guests into the house. "Why don't we sit in the parlor? There's coffee and chocolate chip cookies. Not homemade, unfortunately, but the bakery in town is always good."

They all took seats, Brendan next to Callie on the sofa, Miss Aggie in an overstuffed chair. Callie filled her aunt's pretty porcelain cups with coffee and passed them around, and Miss Aggie helped herself to cookies. At least five of them vanished in her direction.

"I told Miss Aggie a little of what's been going on," Brendan said. "She knows the story. Hell, everyone in Sweet Springs County knows the story of Brendan and Priscilla. It's kind of the old west version of Romeo and Juliet except with a happy ending."

"Or mostly happy," Miss Aggie said. "They had a long, happy life, but the end wasn't so good for Brendan. A problem came up at the ranch. While he was gone, Priscilla took a turn for the worst. She died while he was away. As the story goes, he never forgave himself. He died a few months after she did."

Callie set her cup and saucer down on the coffee table. "I know it sounds crazy, but I think he might still be here."

Miss Aggie smiled. "To someone like me, it doesn't sound crazy at all." She finished the last of her cookie and heaved her big bulk up from the chair. "I'm going to take a walk. I'll be back." She didn't say more, just lumbered off down the hall.

Callie's gaze went to Brendan. "I didn't think I'd hear from you

41

again."

A faint smile touched his lips. "Because of the ghost?"

"Most guys wouldn't want anything to do with a woman who thinks she lives in a house with a ghost."

"You don't seem like the kind of person who goes around making up stories. Plus, there's the dead man on the stairs and no prints, no DNA, nothing. In this day and age, that's not easy to do."

"That's sort of what I was thinking."

"Miss Aggie's been a friend of the family for years. I went to see her to ask her opinion. She said she wanted to see for herself."

Callie hadn't seen the woman go upstairs, but she watched her making her way carefully back down. She looked different somehow, calmer, an oddly vacant expression on her face.

"Have you got any candles?" she asked.

"Of course. In case the power goes off. I'll get them." Callie returned with an assortment of candles. She set two of them on the coffee table and one on the oak sideboard against the wall. Brendan pulled a small box of wooden matches out of his jeans and lit them. It gave the living room a soft eerie glow.

"Be patient," Miss Aggie said. "He's here. I could feel him."

Callie's heart began to pound. Brendan flashed her a glance but made no comment. He reached over and caught her hand, steadying her.

They sat in silence for half an hour, by the antique mantel clock. It was strangely peaceful, until the candle flames started to flicker, and Callie felt the sensation of a big hand sliding beneath her hair, settling possessively around the nape of her neck.

It wasn't Brendan, whose hand still held hers. Callie made a little sound in her throat that drew his attention. His expression changed as he watched the dark curls move, though no one else was touching her.

"I know you're here, Brendan," Miss Aggie said. "And I know why you came. But the lady in the house isn't Priscilla. She looks like your Silla, but her name is Callie. Your Priscilla has gone on to the other side. She's waiting for you there. She misses you terribly. She's been waiting a very long time."

The candle on the sideboard flickered and went out.

"It's true," Miss Aggie said. "She was gone when you came home, but you can find her again. You don't have to live without her.

You just have to look for the light. Do you see it, Brendan?"

A loud whooshing sound filled the room, stirring the draperies.

"Callie belongs to the Brendan of this time. He'll take care of her. He'll protect her."

In the candlelight, Brendan's features looked hard. He glanced at Miss Aggie, who nodded. "Callie's mine," he said. "She belongs to me. She's mine to protect. I give you my solemn pledge that I will."

Callie's heart was beating. Brendan sounded like he meant every word.

"Go on now," Miss Aggie said. "Move toward the light. Go and find your Priscilla. She's waiting. She loves you. Just the way you love her."

The house began to shake, rattling the windows, jiggling the antique stemware in the glass curio case. A sudden burst of light lit the room, so bright Callie had to close her eyes.

Brendan's hand tightened around hers. "Jesus," he said.

A roaring began, rising to a crescendo. The bright light flashed again and something whooshed past them. A fierce crack sounded, then a long heavy roll, like lightning followed by thunder.

Silence fell. The old house slowly settled. Brendan drew Callie into his arms and she felt a tremor run through his hard body.

"It's over," Miss Aggie said. "He won't be back." She smiled. "He's found her again after all these years."

Callie turned her face into Brendan's chest and started to cry.

Epilogue

It was the biggest social event in Sweet Springs that year. The wedding of Sheriff Brendan Trask to the town's new resident, Callie Sutton. Those that couldn't make it to the ceremony in the little white church showed up for the party out at the ranch. Bets were made how long it would take before the first little Trask was born.

Not long, Callie figured, considering how much practice they got. She grinned.

The ghost of the outlaw Trask had never reappeared. Callie firmly believed he was happy with his beloved Priscilla on the other side.

The search for the man who had killed the Red Rose Rapist eventually came to an end. Brendan let the case fade away on its own accord. Though he never mentioned it again, like Callie, he believed the outlaw Brendan had saved Callie that night.

All was well in the little town of Sweet Springs.

Callie believed, at last, all was well on the other side, too.

4

THE BLUFF

Tina DeSalvo

Chapter One

"Hey, Mike. Has a gentleman by the name of Sam O'Leary checked in, yet?"

Seated on the burgundy, velvet settee in the lobby of the Meyers Hotel, Samantha O'Leary heard her father's name and nervously lifted her eyes from the journal she'd been pretending to read. She'd been trying to draw both courage and comfort from her father's large, distinct penmanship–not the actual words, which she knew by heart. She did not understand all of it, but nevertheless had it memorized. His scripted letters were much like him, bold, strong and playful. He'd always been a source of strength, comfort and love for Samantha. Since his death, she missed him with a deep ache–even though she was a bit angry with him, too.

"Nope. He hasn't checked in, Cade," the clerk said, looking up at the formidable man whose back was to her. He filled out his tailored, midnight-black jacket with well-formed muscles, broad shoulders, and a confident posture.

Cade.

He had to be Mr. Caden Parker. The man Sam had traveled all this way–exhausting all her resources–to meet. The man she had lied to by omission because she had no choice. Well, no choice she was willing to take.

Mouth dry, her heart raced, and beneath her kid gloves, her hands grew damp with nervous perspiration. Lying to him was much easier when they'd been corresponding via a few brief telegrams. The reality of what she'd planned suddenly hit her and felt dangerously impossible. How in God's creation had she deluded herself into thinking she could pull–off pretending to be her recently deceased father, or at least, pretending to do his work? She was no more a ghost chaser than she was a buffalo skinner.

Her father was known, by those who knew such things, as the most accomplished ghost chaser in America. He had made an excellent living traveling around the country getting rid of ghosts in people's homes, barns, businesses, and, in one case, an outhouse. She had merely worked as his assistant–communicating with clients and arranging travel for him so he could communicate and arrange travel for the ghosts. She also took care of his accounting, stocking his supplies and running his household. Never had she actually expelled a ghost with him. He preferred to work alone.

Well, I'm going to have to do it this time.

This one time.

She'd exhausted all her options. She had no other choice. With no time to find another way to earn the funds, she had to collect the fee for this job. Had to. Her very successful, beloved papa had left her penniless and on the brink of losing her home, because he was not so successful at the poker table. *Oh, Papa...*

Heart pounding, knees wobbling, Sam stood and walked to the tall man in unrelieved black, from felt Stetson to leather boots. Resisting the urge to make sure her defiant, red curls remained pinned at the back of her head, she locked her knees and lifted her chin to face six-feet-plus of focused, powerful male virility and good looks. "I'm Sam O'Leary," she managed to say with the force and confidence her father would've used.

She'd never considered herself a coward, but right now in this moment, as Mr. Parker assessed her with the bluest eyes under the darkest lashes Sam had ever seen, she felt like the most courageous woman in the world–for not picking up her skirts and running away.

Pulling back her shoulders, journal tucked beneath her arm, she extended her hand. He took off his right, black leather glove, and

46

engulfed her hand. A vibrating sort of warmth seemed to spark from his long, lean fingers and palm against hers. Her insides ignited into a burning heat, like she'd stepped inside of a freshly stoked fire.

Was that heat from fear? Stress? The entire situation scared her to death. Yet she knew instinctively that her physical reaction hadn't come from fear. It was because of Mr. Parker the man, not the client, that her body was behaving in a way it never had before today. Of course, she'd never been under such stress, prior to having to deal with her current dire financial situation.

"You certainly aren't what I was expecting, *Sam* O'Leary." He tilted his head, revealing shiny black curls beneath his hat.

"Oh? Am I shorter than you expected?" She politely pulled her hand from his without resistance.

His laugh came quick and honest. "That, too, I suppose." There was a rough, mischievous tone to his laugh in contrast to the hint of his sophisticated northeastern accent. He may have had the posture and stance of the tough men of the west, but it was obvious his roots weren't from here.

She smiled, surprised that she managed to joke with him and enjoy it when she had so much on the line.

"And I hadn't expected you to be so pretty… with fiery hair and sparkling emerald eyes… so beautiful… " he hesitated and looked her directly in the eyes, "so female."

"Well, for what it's worth, the male Sam O'Leary, my father, was also a redhead with green eyes." She smiled. "And a thick, graying beard."

"Well, at least your beard isn't turning gray."

Her hand flew to her face. "What? I don't have a beard."

He lifted her chin gently with his finger and pretended to examine her face. "No, you do not." She gently pushed his hand away and took a step back, needing to put a little more space between them. He hooked his thumbs onto his smooth, leather gun belt slung around his waist. His gun, holstered on the belt, was worn like his wool pants. Snug against his leg. "So, you're Sam."

"Short for Samantha," she said, not bothering to tell him that until her father died, she'd never used Sam as a nickname.

Nor had she ever claimed to be a ghost chaser.

He nodded, and his smile faded. "Well, *Miss Sam*," he began, his voice even, serious, "if I'd known you were a woman, I wouldn't have hired you."

His bluntness surprised her, but his response wasn't unexpected. "Well, you did hire me." His brow lifted. She rushed on, not giving him a chance to fire her on the spot and send her back to New Orleans. Even if he reimbursed her for the expenses she'd incurred— she'd had to sell the family grandfather clock to pay for the trip— she'd lose her home.

Her father had put up their house as collateral for a note he had used to secure a place at a big poker game. She found out about it when he died–an hour before the game was to be played. She needed to earn the fee to buy back the note.

"If you didn't want a woman to do the job, you should've asked me my gender before you hired me. If you had, I would have told you." She crossed her fingers behind her back. "There's no problem here, Mr. Parker. Women have proven to make better ghost hunters than men, which is why I was my father's top pupil." *Well, not really his pupil.* "My gender should not bother you."

"Bother?" He smiled again, and her heart seemed to flip in her chest. "No, that isn't the word that pops into mind when I look at you." He touched the back of her arm and guided her back to the settee she'd just vacated. When she did, he took the seat next to her– closer than she would've liked, but his long legs ate up most of the room.

"Miss Sam, the problem with you being female is that the… " he glanced around to make sure no one was listening, "… the ghost seems to only haunt the women at the Bluff."

"The Bluff?"

"I don't have anything against working women," he continued, ignoring her question. "I'm sure you're good at what you do. You came highly recommended from a friend in Savannah who had a problem …"

"In his attic. A little boy who liked to play marbles all night."

He smiled. "Yes. That's what he said. A satisfied customer who now can sleep through the night." He lowered his voice to just above a silky whisper. "He didn't tell me how attractive you are. Surprising, really." She blushed and his smile faded. "This situation is very different from my friend's. I'm not sure you're right for the job."

Samantha's throat tightened. She had to be right or she'd be homeless in less than a week. "Mr. Parker, are you a man of your word or not? We have an agreement." She kept her voice steady and her eyes in contact with his. "My qualifications are the same as when you hired me. I began working with my late father when my mother passed. I was six. That's twenty years." Stick to the truth as much as possible, she reminded herself, just as planned. "I know all of his strategies and protocol… " She'd read them in his journal and knew some from dinner conversations. She had actually seen him performing the first protocol on two occasions when a ghost happened into the room as they were having an initial meeting with clients.

"There's a protocol for this sort of thing?" When he smiled, she found herself smiling back. Butterflies began to take flight in her stomach.

"Certainly. Some consider it a science." She thought of all the things her father had done, and of all of the herbs and items she was charged with keeping stocked in his traveling trunk.

"Ghosts and science." He shook his head.

She looked past him, out the window to their right. Snow still sat in small, melting mounds between the boardwalk and the sun-dried dirt road of Main Street. Looking at the end-of-season snow and seeing the late afternoon breeze playing havoc with dresses and jackets of those walking by had Samantha grabbing the edges of her cream shawl and tightening it around her shoulders.

"Cold?"

"It looks cold outside."

"When the ghost is in the room doing his haunting, I'm told you know where he is by the cold spots." He shrugged. "I haven't felt it, mind you, but others claim to feel his presence when he's near." He paused and appeared to be trying to formulate something that was weighing on his mind. "I think you should know, Miss Sam," he continued, "I'm just going through the motions of getting rid of the ghost because the ladies have to get back to work. I want them to think the ghost is gone." He looked deep into her eyes. She understood he wasn't seeking approval or expecting rejection. "Quite frankly, I don't believe in ghosts."

I don't blame you, Mr. Parker. I don't believe in ghosts either.

She'd never utter those thoughts aloud. Ever. Never had. To confess it would be to accuse her father of being a charlatan. And, she didn't believe he was. He had sincerely and without a doubt believed in ghosts. Believed in them and spoke of them as if they were real people. His clients believed too, and were extraordinarily satisfied with his services. She couldn't reconcile that the man she had loved most in the world was a believer when she was not. So, she didn't. He was a good man and his clients adored him. That was good enough for her.

"Ladies?" she asked, as his statement completely registered. "What ladies are you talking about? Your mother? Sister? Wife?"

"No. I'm single and my family still lives in Philadelphia. I'm talking about the dancers and painted ladies who work at the Bluff. It's my saloon and gambling hall."

Saloon? Gambling Hall? She'd taken a job in the exact type of place that ruined her life. She snapped her agape mouth shut and tried to wipe away any shock that might show on her face.

"Not where you expected to be working, huh?" Cade rested his elbows on his knees. "So, you see, this is why you being a female Sam, and not a male Sam, is a problem, Miss O'Leary. You not only dress like a proper, Christian woman, you carry yourself like one. That tells me that you won't cotton to helping the disreputable working ladies in my saloon."

Well, her father would've certainly taken a job to eradicate a ghost in a saloon, then stayed afterwards to play poker in its gambling hall.

Could this job be any more difficult? Dear God, I would've preferred dealing with a dozen ghosts in a dirty old outhouse. But, what choice do I have?

"As a female, I'm the perfect person for the job, Mr. Parker." She stiffened her spine and her resolve. "I will rid the Bluff of the ghost that's haunting women there. I'll begin tonight." She stood. "Good day."

She walked away without a backward glance. There was a lot of planning to do. She had to figure out how to get rid of a ghost she and her client didn't believe existed.

Chapter Two

"We will begin with Protocol Number One," Samantha told his six female employees who'd gathered upstairs in one of the dollar-a-night rooms Cade rented to saloon patrons who'd rather stay closer to the action than in one of Two Moon Junction's hotels. She'd selected this particular room to set up her trunk full of her ghost-fighting supplies because the girls had told her the ghost had never haunted them in there. Cade had no clue why that should matter. Nor did he care as long as the pretty ghost chaser with the creamy skin, expressive green eyes and flaming red hair kept his popular employees working.

Samantha O'Leary was a real pleasure to look at. She was damn intriguing too. He didn't remember ever meeting a woman who had caught his attention more. Even now, as she stood there wearing the ridiculous stained, white shirt that was six times too big for her. The man's shirt, worn like a coat over a conservative dark green-black skirt and pleated blouse the color of morning fog, didn't lessen her beauty. In fact, it only accentuated her tiny waist, full breasts, and soft feminine curves.

She opened the trunk, and the ladies, dressed in their bright magenta, purple and black satin and lace costumes, fell completely silent. They sat up taller, stretching their necks, or outright moved closer to look inside the large leather trunk.

Cade peered over them to get a look, too. Oh hell. It was filled with a bunch of shiny rocks, crystals, and bags of herbs—if his sense of smell was accurate. Yeah, he definitely smelled sage, cayenne, and dill. There was even some Spanish moss poking out from one of the bags.

It was a carnival show. He expected juggling balls to tumble onto the floor at any moment.

He crossed his arms over his chest and leaned against the wall next to the closed door leading to the hall. He'd give Samantha credit. Her confidence and powerful take-charge attitude had won the ladies over... just like it had won him over earlier that day in the hotel lobby when his intention had been to send her packing.

Her adorable determination, her sweet smile, her faint air of desperation had made him decide to give her a chance. What harm could it do?

Unlike himself, his girls believed she could actually get rid of their ghost.

"What is Protocol Number One?" That question from his youngest saloon dancer, eighteen-year-old Darling Dotty. The pretty and energetic brunette was the one who had given the ghost his nickname: Mad Murray. The girls were all convinced that the ghost was the perverted slug he'd won the saloon from after a long, hard-fought poker game five months ago. Murray Hopkins had disappeared from Two Moon Junction just a week after he'd turned over the deed to the saloon. He'd been drunk damn near all the time since he lost the saloon, so no one knew for sure if he just wandered out of town or met his death–accidentally or otherwise. Cade was just glad he was gone. The so-called hauntings started a week after his disappearance. At first it was small incidents, an object being moved from a dresser onto a bed, to more troubling episodes involving cold spots and strange sounds.

"In Protocol One, I simply ask Mr. Murray to leave." Samantha placed her hands on her hips, the bedsheet-sized dirty shirt bunched in folds beneath her hands. "I know it sounds oversimplified, but it works. You just have to use the right tone and tell him why he needs to leave." She glanced at Cade and quickly looked back to the women. Did she expect him to back her up on that ridiculous claim or renounce it? He did neither. This was her show, not his. "If you see him or know he's around, call me immediately. I'll confront him."

"He ain't going to take no orders from no woman," said Anna, the oldest of the three saloon dancers, looking horrified. She pointed the horsehair brush she'd been using to tame her wiry, brown hair at Samantha. "I hope you have another protocol to use on him. He's mean, Samantha. Mean and stubborn."

All of the women started speaking at one time.

"He's cruel."

"He appears when we're helpless. Naked or gettin' undressed."

"It's scary."

"I felt him touch my ass." All their voices overlapping–except Sarah. She seemed to disappear within herself whenever Mad Murray was mentioned.

Anna stood now, not bothering to adjust her black and red lace work dress that had folded up on one side to show well-muscled dancers' legs above her knees. "I hope you know what you're doin'." She walked to the door, pausing to speak to Cade. All of the other women stopped speaking and looked at her. "I'm goin' to work now. If she doesn't get rid of him, I can't keep hangin' around. He's gettin' bolder. He's goin' to hurt me... us." She opened the door, but didn't leave.

Not good. The girls seemed to take their cue from her more

than they didn't. "Give the ghost chaser a chance," he offered.

She looked at him, her dark eyes unblinking. "I cain't afford to take chances." She turned and left.

The other girls looked at Samantha. He saw hope, concern, and doubt in their eyes. He also saw that they wanted reassuring.

"There are many protocols," she said to the women. Again, there was a strength and confidence in her tone and in the way she held her body. "We always start with number one. If it doesn't work, we learn and move forward. Ladies, I need y'all to be strong and have positive thoughts. Believe. My father always told me that belief is more than half the battle."

The women nodded. Some even smiled at her. "We trust you, Samantha," Betty, his most popular painted dove, told her. She had a kind heart, but she'd had a tough life that gave her a rough edge too. "Just don't take too long, you hear? We need to work and the customers are noticing how jumpy we are. They don't like skittish women and some have already gone to other working women in town."

"I understand how important it is to earn your way," she said, and Cade thought she sounded the most honest and vulnerable he'd heard her in their short acquaintance. A quick glance at Betty and the ladies who were looking at Samantha told him they sensed it too.

* * *

Five pair of eyes looked at her with such hopefulness that it took Samantha's breath away. Dear Lord, it hurt her insides to know she was lying to these people who were counting on her to get their lives back on track. She turned her back to them, adjusting the bundles of herbs in the bags on the shelves laddered inside the trunk, needing a moment to gather her courage. She understood how they were holding on by a thread, making a living the best way they could. Like she was, only her thread was frayed so thin, a slight breeze might sever it.

Breathe, Samantha. Remember you can help them through this rough spot, just like they're helping you. You aren't so different from them.

It was in that second, with that thought, that she vowed to do just that. Help these believers to believe their horrible ghost was gone.

She turned, holding a bag of juniper, and felt Cade's eyes on her.

She didn't dare look at him; her heart and stomach acted very strangely when she did. On some level, she understood that eventually she had to take a moment to think about why her body involuntarily reacted to him this way, and why she really liked being around him. But not now.

"Tonight, after I ask Murray to leave, we'll burn this juniper," she told the women. She took a sniff of the piney herb and handed it to Sarah. Sarah's eyes widened and she took a sniff before handing it to Betty. "Juniper is known to clear out spirits."

"We'll need it to get rid of Mad Murray's stink," Dotty laughed, handing the bag back to Samantha.

"You didn't mention him smelling bad before." Samantha placed the juniper back into the trunk.

"He smells awful." Betty snorted.

"Just like he did when he was alive," Sarah said, her voice just above a whisper. Samantha waited for Sarah to say more. She sensed that she didn't speak of Murray much, but should. Something in her sad eyes told her there was more to this fear of Murray than him being a ghost. "He smells of cheap cigars, the whiskey he spilled on his clothes because he was too drunk to lift his glass to his lips… and hate."

"He didn't bathe much either," Dotty offered. "I think he was afraid of water. It was perfect that he… "

"It was perfectly disgusting," Betty jumped in, finishing her sentence.

If Samantha hadn't been looking at Sarah when Dotty spoke, she might have missed the wild look that came into her eyes.

"I have to go," Betty said, shouting over her shoulder as she rushed out the door. "I left a customer in my room and he'll be ready for another go about now."

Fifteen minutes later after all of the ladies' questions were answered, Dotty stood. "Let's get to work, girls. I hear a crowd gathering downstairs. Let's see if we can get a few gents friendly and generous with their coin."

"That went well," Samantha told Cade once they were alone.

"Well?" He smiled and shook his head. "You're an optimistic sort."

"No reason not to be." She shrugged, knowing she had to believe she would succeed, save her home, and not end up working in a saloon like the women who had just left the room. She was a terrible dancer… and a virgin. Her thoughts turned to Sarah. "What happened to Sarah?"

Cade walked to the window and looked outside. "Sarah is skittish… "

"And, so sad." Samantha took a few moments to close the trunk before continuing. "Something really bad happened to her." She turned toward Cade, who no longer stood in front of the window, but had moved closer to her. The frigid mountain air that blew into the room from the window he'd opened, sending the cotton curtains lifting up like sheets drying on a clothesline, didn't seem to bother him.

"These ladies all have sad stories. Tough lives."

Samantha nodded, rubbing her chilled arms. "Yes, they do."

"What's your story, Sam–Samantha?"

What was he asking and why was he asking it? Nothing in the depths of his beautiful blue eyes told her. They seemed to make her insides sizzle with heat and electricity, like lightning striking the tallest tree. "Nothing extraordinary."

He took a step closer. "I would bet that isn't true."

"I'm guessing you bet on many things."

"You would be wrong."

"But you're a gambler."

"I play cards… well. Very well."

"Don't all gamblers, um, I mean, card players, think that?"

He shrugged. "They wouldn't all be right. I am."

The cold now seemed to seep into her bones. "My papa thought he was too." Why had she admitted that? She shook her head. "What time does Murray usually arrive?"

"So, your father gambled," he said, ignoring her question. "Poorly, I gather."

"Yes, Mr. Parker. He gambled… poorly." Once again, she rubbed the chill that rushed across her flesh. "Do you mind if I close the window? I'm not used to the cold."

Cade moved closer to her and rubbed his strong palms along her arms. Warmth from more than his ministrations took the chill from her body. "Sam, the window is closed."

Samantha jerked her head to look at the window. The curtains lay still. "I didn't see you close it."

"It was never opened." He lifted her chin to look into her eyes. "Are you okay?"

Before she could answer or figure out what trick he was playing on her, there was a scream from somewhere down the hall.

Chapter Three

"He touched my thigh," Betty shouted as soon as Samantha rushed into her room. She stood next to her bed, pale and wearing a satin skirt and black bustier, her heavy breasts spilling from the top. "He ran cold, bony fingers on my thighs." She shivered, grabbing the quilt from the bed to wrap around her shoulders.

"I didn't touch her, yet," the man sitting in his long johns on the edge of the bed yelled. "So, what if I did? I paid for her."

Samantha's face heated as she turned away from the toothless man, indecently dressed, but not before she saw Cade hand the man a gold coin and get a gummy smile in return. "This should cover your trouble." Cade handed him his clothes and led him out of the room.

"He's still here," Betty whispered, shivering. "I smell him." She looked at Samantha, eyes wide. "You smell him, don't you?"

Samantha did not.

"There," Betty pointed near the window. "I see a... different light, there."

Samantha looked to the window, but saw nothing. Of course, she didn't. There was no ghost there. There was no such thing as ghosts.

"Mr. Hopkins," Samantha said, walking to the window, remembering the exact instructions on how to do Protocol Number One. "I'm Samantha O'Leary. Daughter of the late Sam O'Leary. I want you to leave this room, this saloon, this world." She kept her voice even. Calm. It was easy when she didn't think the ghost was actually there.

"He's by the door," Betty pointed across the room. Cade opened the door and walked in. Betty's mouth fell open. Samantha rushed to her side and held her hand.

"Remember, have calm, positive thoughts, Betty. Believe he will leave."

"Calm? Are you crazy?" She sucked in a breath and let out a heavy exhale. "Okay."

"Mr. Hopkins," Samantha continued, "you don't belong here.

You've passed away, now you must pass to the other side. Go to the light." She had no idea what light her father referred to in his journal, but she repeated what he'd written. "Be at peace. Leave. Now. You don't belong here anymore."

Betty looked at her, her lips quivering, the quilt hanging on her shoulders. Samantha smiled. Cade ran his hand over his mouth, his eyes bright with humor. Was he covering a smile? Samantha narrowed her eyes to scold him, to stop him if he was. He shrugged and winked at her.

Betty sniffed the air. "I think he's gone." Her voice was soft, but hopeful. "I don't smell him or see that strange ghost light."

"Yes. He's gone. It's over." She hugged Betty.

A scream sounded from another room down the hall.

* * *

Samantha's heart pounded in her ears as she ran full steam down the hall, trying to identify where the latest scream came from. "I can't tell who's screaming. She sounds really scared. Oh Cade, it sounds like it's coming from a cave."

Cade grabbed her hand while drawing his gun with his free hand, pausing in front of each door. Betty was right behind them, crying, "It sounds like Dotty."

Dotty appeared at the top of the stairs. Her face pale, but she wasn't screaming.

"Wait here with the girls," he told Samantha. "Right here." He waved for Dotty to stand with Samantha and Betty.

She wanted to go with him, felt she should, felt she'd be safer if she did. But she also felt she should stay there to protect Betty and Dotty. How she'd protect them, she didn't know. Cade disappeared down the stairs and the screaming grew louder, more frightening. All three women covered their ears.

"Make it stop," Dotty cried.

Samantha had no idea how to do that. Never had she felt more like a fraud than she did now. God, she hated being helpless; she began to pray. Betty and Dotty started praying with her. She knew she needed to do more and looked down the hall, opposite the stairs where Cade had gone. There was a window, the curtains blowing wildly as the curtains had when she was with Cade. Her stomach pinched. She looked more closely at the window. It was closed.

"Stay here," she told Betty and Dotty, who were now on their knees, clinging to one another.

"Do you think Mad Murray has Sarah again?" she heard Dotty ask Betty as she headed to the window. "She won't survive it this time."

"He's dead. His ghost body can't hurt her the same way. Be quiet," Betty shouted. "Keep praying."

The closer Samantha got to the window, the colder it got. She ignored the painfully icy chill along her skin beneath her sleeves and stopped in front of the window. She was so frightened her legs could barely hold her up. She wanted to run from the building into the street, away from the god-awful screaming, the cold, and the frightening billowing of the curtains. But she was here to do a job: help Cade, Betty, Dotty, Anna, Sarah, and the rest of the ladies.

"I don't believe in ghosts," she whispered. "This is a trick—something easily explained or something complicated, but still a trick."

She pressed her hands along the edges of the window, searching for a source of the airflow that had the curtains flapping like flags on a pole. No air. Just the frigid cold that felt like it was seeping into her bones. Then suddenly, the curtains drifted down and were still. "Who are you?" she asked, her voice sounding shaky. There was a flutter of the curtain on her right and she turned toward it and her papa's shirt puffed up around her. "Oh God, what is going on? I know you're not a ghost."

The curtain appeared to be normal again, just a little more wrinkled than the one on the left. Her heart raced harder, faster. No. Not wrinkled. Something else. Her shirt puffed again and then she saw it.

"Papa?"

The curtain was flat in some places and raised in others, forming the silhouette of her father's body. It was undeniable. His thick midsection, broad shoulders, and Irish upturned nose. Even where his thick beard jutted off his chin onto his chest there was a fullness and depression in the curtain fabric.

"Papa!" Her heart leaped.

She reached for the curtain, wanting to hug her papa, feel his strength, but the material just slid through her fingers. No. He wasn't there. It was her imagination. The frayed nerves from the screams and the crying hysterics from Dotty and Betty had her mind playing tricks on her.

The curtain moved again. It looked like her papa shaking his head no. Then what looked like his thick arm rose, a finger at the end of it pointed to the room she was in with the ladies earlier. "Your trunk is in there. Do you want me to go to the trunk, Papa?"

The curtains went flat.

She shivered. Not from fear. Her papa wouldn't harm her nor send her into harm's way. Tears filled her eyes. "I miss you, Papa." Her heart ached with pride and the knowledge that he wanted to help her and the people from the Bluff.

"Dotty. Betty. Follow me."

She led them into the room with her papa's trunk. It was open. The bags of sage, rosemary, and galangal were lying on its side on the interior shelves, while the other herbs remained neatly stacked as she'd left them. Matches seemed knocked over as well.

She knew her papa wanted her to create an incense with these specific herbs. She'd read about them in his journal. These were used to chase away evil or malicious spirits.

Samantha instructed Betty and Dotty to bunch the herbs together into three bundles and tie the twine on the shelf around the ends. Then she lit one of them, blowing lightly on the end to put out the flame, leaving a steady stream of smoke in its stead.

Cade walked into the room, looked at what she held in her hand, and nodded.

"This ghost is evil," she told him, handing him the smoldering herbs. "Use big sweeping strokes and cleanse the room with it. Make sure you face each wall."

A small, brass bell fell off the shelf with a tinny ring. Samantha picked it up and handed it to Dotty. "Take it and ring it in each corner. It will do the same thing as the smoke. Then you and Betty go into each room of the saloon upstairs and down and do it there."

She lit the other bundles. "Cade, come with me. We need to cleanse the entire saloon."

"Darling, you know I don't believe in all this voodoo, ghost stuff." He smiled. "But I believe in you."

He kissed her on the cheek and went to work.

Chapter Four

With each room they cleansed, the screams decreased until finally it stopped.

"You did it," Cade shouted, hugging her to him, and turning her in a fast, tight circle. "I knew you could."

She laughed, throwing her head back. "No, you didn't."

He kissed her on top of the head. "You're right, I thought you were the worst ghost chaser in the history of your crazy, fraudulent ghost-chasing profession."

She laughed. "I don't blame you, Cade. I was pretty awful."

"Not awful at all," Betty shouted, running down the stairs. "You got rid of Mad Murray!"

Dotty and Anna and the rest of the ladies came rushing into the saloon, laughing. Sarah followed them and even she was smiling. Samantha moved away from Cade and went up to the women, hugging each of them.

"He's gone now," she told them. "Murray was so mean that his ghost wasn't willing to leave y'all alone, even after y'all... he was killed."

They stopped celebrating and looked at her. "You know?" Anna asked.

She shook her head. "Not the details, but I know he probably died while doing something awful to either one or more of you." They looked at Sarah first, then one another. She had tears in her eyes. "My guess is that he blamed y'all for his death, but the real blame lies with him. Never doubt that."

"We don't," Betty said.

"Should I be asking what this is all about?" Cade looked from Sam to the women and back again.

They shook their heads, "no", but said nothing more about it. This was one truth that would be a secret to take to their graves.

Chilly air rushed through Samantha's father's shirt again and she laughed. "Is puffing up your old shirt how we'll communicate from now on, Papa?"

"I hope not," Cade said, walking up behind her and pulling her back to his chest. "I hate that ugly shirt." She turned in his arms to face him.

"Does that mean you believe in ghosts now?"

"Hell no." He smiled. "But I've come to believe in other things I didn't before I met you."

"For example?"

"A crazy thing called love at first sight."

He pulled her tighter to him and she felt his heart pounding against her breasts, as hard as hers was beneath them. Did she really hear him say he believed in love at first sight? Did that mean he loved her? Was it love that had turned her body into fire and sparking electricity when she was around him? Had she fallen in love with him at first sight too?

She didn't need her papa puffing up his old shirt to give her an answer she already knew deep in her heart.

"So you believe in love at first sight too, huh?"

"Yeah. I love you, my crazy ghost chaser." His eyes widened, and he stepped back. "Did you say 'too'?"

She nodded. "I love you, Caden Parker."

Her shirt puffed, and she felt a hard push from behind her, knocking her back into his arms. "Okay, Papa. I know. I know." Cade looked at her, his brow cocked. "I owe you the whole truth, though, Cade. All of it. If I don't, my papa will never leave me alone."

He lifted his other brow.

"You're not the only one who doesn't believe in ghosts. Well, I didn't until an hour ago."

"Are you kidding me?" His laugh was loud and full. "I hired a ghost chaser who didn't believe in ghosts? You're a bold one, Sam. Very bold. You just pulled the biggest bluff I've ever been part of. I respect that."

She laughed. "You would. There's a reason for that… "

"I know about you needing money to buy back your father's note to keep your house," Cade said. "When I discovered you were a woman, and not the man I expected, I did a little checking. It only took two telegrams and one hour to find out about your financial problems." He reached inside his suit pocket and handed her a folded document. "That's the deed to your house. It's yours, Samantha."

She clutched the deed to her chest, and her shirt started flapping madly. "You did that for me… "

"Love at first sight, darlin'." He laughed. "Now, please tell your papa to leave us alone so I can kiss you like a man who loves his woman should."

5

DYING TO SEE

An Exposed Series Story

Jennifer St. Giles

"Love will find a way through paths where wolves fear to prey."
-Lord Byron

The seconds on the clock ticked faster and grew louder with each passing moment, marking impending doom, like a timer on a bomb. Venus, red hair flowing wildly, fled through the mountain mists. Fear in her every movement. Desperation in her every breath.

In the shadows of a moonless night, a mammoth wolf closed in fast, ravenous fangs ready for the kill.

"Here!" the warrior shouted, rushing uphill to her, his sword raised to save her from the beast." Come this way!"

Venus ran, never turning toward him, blinded by her fear.

He fought harder and screamed louder.

The wolf shifted its massive head his way, its golden gaze and feral jowls gleamed in satisfaction before swiftly moving in for the kill.

"Here! Come after me!" The wolf ignored him. Heart hammering, the warrior threw his sword in desperation. His only hope to pierce the wolf's side. The sword arced through the air but passed through the beast instead of killing it.

"No!" The warrior shouted in agony. He and his armament weren't real.

The wolf knocked Venus to the ground, pouncing on her. She turned to fight but had no chance against the beast's power. In one feral strike, he ripped her throat—

Devin St. Claire struggled against the vision, not wanting to see the rest, but his curse held him captive, an unwilling witness to the wolf's savagery.

Crying out, Devin rolled from his bed, sickened to his soul. His pulse pounded. His chest hurt, and his stomach knotted with pain.

Sweat drenched his skin. He stood, gasping for air, straining to see beyond the darkness of the night and his encroaching blindness. Each day, he woke dying to see every nuance of the world around him one more time. A genetic disease—retinitis pigmentosa—eroded his peripheral vision year after year.

Shaking off the images, he tried to tell himself he'd had a nightmare. He knew the "Venus" well, and not a moment passed that he didn't yearn for her.

But he'd let her go, forced her away. Cursing, he fisted his hands and drew a deep breath. He had too much time on his hands and had been listening too much to the music she loved. Every blues song he played only made Devin want her more. He needed to end his sabbatical and return to the concert stage.

Music always eased his soul and was the one part of his life where sight didn't matter. When the day came where he couldn't see the notes, he could play well by ear. After breaking with Caroline, he hadn't the heart for anything lately but heartbreak blues. He spent too much time remembering her.

She wanted a family and deserved a man who could give her healthy children. He'd never curse a son with his blindness. And he'd never curse a child with his visions, or any of the other "psychic gifts" the St. Claire's unfailingly inherited.

No point in trying to talk himself out of what just happened. He'd had a vision of the future; one that filled him with dread. Moving to his dresser, he found the framed photo of him and Dr. Caroline Ward in Venice. Frowning, he picked up the photo and the heavy silver cross wrapped around it, his heart thudding. His grandfather was the last to wear the St. Claire Cross. He used it for protection against the demons he fought. The necklace had been passed down from generation to generation in his family, but Devin had never worn it. He always kept it in its protective box at the back of his drawer.

Had Iris or Eva been in his room? Or had their sergeant housekeeper, Lannie, been cleaning? He almost returned the cross to its box, but, at the urging in his gut, he slipped the thick necklace on instead then focused on the picture.

Before ending their relationship, he'd taken Caro to every place he'd ever dreamed of going so he could store the memory in his mind. One day, he would barely be able to see the photographs of their time together.

"Devin! Are you okay?" His sister Eva knocked hard on the door to his room. He lived with his two sisters in the family's Victorian-style mansion, not far from Atlanta, Georgia. You would think with over six-thousand square feet of living space he'd have some privacy. No such luck. Before he could slip the picture back, Eva burst into the room. She took one look at him and winced. "What did you see?"

He considered lying, but knew between Eva's sharp eye and his other sister, Iris's telepathy, they'd piece his vision together. With Caroline being Iris's psychiatrist, she'd identify his "Venus" by her red hair in a heartbeat. He set the photograph on his dresser and faced Eva. "Depending on how much of the vision is literal and how much is allegorical, I either foresaw Caroline's gruesome murder, or one of life's wolves—like cancer—will eat her alive."

Eva exhaled hard and leaned against the doorjamb. "You need to call her. We need to save her without revealing your precognitive abilities. What else did you see?"

"A racing clock," he said grimly, choosing to omit the warrior's efforts to save Venus failed.

"Call her now."

"It's one AM. Everything I've dreamed has always been in the future, not immediate. My vision of Adam dying to save you was weeks ago, and while you both have had close calls, the vision is still hanging over our heads. The premonition of Caroline can likely wait until morning."

"Ever saw a clock before?"

"No."

"Call her."

"Fine." Devin crossed the room, agitation eating at him, because he knew Eva was right. He would have caved to his own worry within a minute or two, but fear had him dragging his heels. When it

65

came to his love for Caroline, he had to be the worse coward in existence. He refused to tell her the truth behind their breakup because he knew she'd talk him out of it. She could undo him and his resolve in a single touch.

Dialing, he waited with growing anxiety as every ring went unanswered until her voicemail picked up.

"Every problem can be solved. Leave me a message, and we'll take care of it." He gritted his teeth as her soothing tones washed over his senses. Even her voicemail tried to undo his convictions. "It's Devin. I need to talk to you as soon as you get this message. Call me." He disconnected, both relieved and worried more.

"I'll get Iris," Eva said.

"Why? I called Caroline's personal line. She always answers it."

"She might know where Dr. Caro could be. Iris saw her on Friday."

Devin nodded. "Meet me in the kitchen. I need a drink." He hated waking Iris. Her harrowing experience this past year had unnerved them all. Being telepathic with little control over the thought waves she picks up, she'd connected twice to the same serial killer. Living his kills through his thoughts nearly drove Iris crazy. She had to be hospitalized both times. Caroline, a top psychiatrist who specialized in post-traumatic stress disorders, stepped in to care for Iris.

To keep the family's psychic gifts in the closet, they blamed Iris's trouble on nightmares. Three-year-old Iris was the only witness to their father killing their mother and himself twenty years ago.

With the serial killer dead, and Iris no longer under his influence and lashing out in a dream-like state, Devin hoped Iris would be free and clear of the sick bastard. She wasn't. He'd spoken to Iris from beyond the grave once. With Iris at the time, Eva heard the demonic voice, too. Everyone now waited for the other ghostly shoe to drop. Maybe finding the cross front and center in his drawer was a supernatural message from his grandfather.

Snagging a shirt, Devin tried to call Caro again at her work number but hung up before reaching her voicemail. *Damn.* If she hadn't always had that as her message, he'd have thought she'd put it up just for him. Her unfailing optimism is one of the things he loved about her. She didn't go about with rose-colored glasses. She saw the brutal reality life dished out to its least and often forgotten, but she did believe every problem when faced head-on and persistently, had some solution to it.

He reached the kitchen, put water onto boil for Eva and Iris's tea, and grabbed a bottle of Macallan 18; his go-to drink for post-vision hell. The Speyside single malt whiskey from the Highlands might not solve his problem, but on occasion, it made swallowing them a bit easier. He saved Macallan 25 for doozies. While he considered his premonition about Caro really bad, he wasn't ready to pull out the big guns yet.

Iris stumbled into the kitchen. He winced at her haunted-eyed look. Iris sat at the table and Eva went to fix tea.

"Dr. Caro is in Lake Tahoe," Iris said.

"Oh," he whispered and frowned as his heart squeezed. *Who had she gone with?* Not that it was any of his business. He'd told her to move on with her life. But Tahoe had been one of their best—make it sexiest—trips. He downed more of his drink than he intended.

"You coward!" Iris, having read his thought, popped from her chair. "You love her, yet continue to turn your back on her. I wish she had gone to Nevada with somebody. Maybe it would wake you up." Incensed, she came at him with her blue gaze sparking fire. For a moment, he braced himself, recalling how she'd lashed out at him last week, trying to kill the serial killer invading her mind. Instead of smacking him now, she snatched the bottle of Macallan.

"Hey!" he reached for his prized whiskey.

She danced away. "We've got a plane to catch. Dr. Caro's in Lake Tahoe for a convention. Though she didn't say, I assumed it's shrink related because she said there were several lectures on the mind's abilities she wanted to hear."

He frowned. Going back to Tahoe and its memories would undo him. "There is no *we* in this. I'll call her hotel room and convince her to come home. Where is she staying?"

"Les Moritz."

That's where they'd stayed together. *Damn.*

"So, what will you say?" Iris demanded. "This is Devin. I've had a vision about your death, and you need to be careful?" His sister's sarcasm hit home. He didn't know what he'd say to Caroline, but realized he had to say it in person.

Putting two cups on the table, Eva topped off the steaming tea with the Macallan. He winced at the waste of the Highland's best.

67

"As crazy as it sounds, Iris is right," Eva said. "The ticking clock can't be ignored. We need to get to Tahoe ASAP. Iris can read thoughts and I can, hell, I don't know, do something."

As an empath, Eva had visions of murders at the crime scenes. He prayed he would never need Eva's skills for Caroline. "No. Absolutely not. I'll go alone. Not only does Iris need more time to recover, but I can't put my full focus on saving Caroline, if I'm worried about you two."

"In your vision, where did the attack happen?" Eva asked.

Devin downed the rest of the whiskey, wishing his vision had been of a sand dune or a city street. "Exactly where she is. Mountainous terrain on a moonless night."

Grim, Eva pulled out her cell. "The new moon starts tomorrow."

His ticking clock had a date.

* * *

Looking like a French village, the five-star Les Moritz, offered every amenity and activity for vacationers. From lakeside villas and hotel to ski slope chalets and lodge, the resort spanned half a mountainside and valley.

Devin paid the driver and exited the car as a bellboy collected his bag. Briefcase in one hand and cane in the other. Easing his cane and his gaze from right to left and left to right as he moved into the hotel.

Usually, Lake Tahoe glistened from Sierra Nevada's lush evergreens like a sapphire amid emeralds, but today a faint haze of smoke dulled its pristine beauty. Wildfires had knocked out several cell towers, limiting all services for the area. His high-tech phone sat useless in his pocket, a frustrating development. Neither his sisters nor Caroline could reach him. All calls to Caroline's room went unanswered. He didn't know if she'd received the messages he'd left for her.

He still didn't know what or how much he'd tell her. He had to stop whatever or whoever the wolf might be from devouring her. When he puzzled out a vision, he stopped bad things from happening. But sometimes, like with his parents' tragedy, he didn't see the truth until afterward.

That guilt overwhelmed him.

His one thread of sanity now, is all his visions were of future events. Caroline had to be safe still.

Flying into the Tahoe Valley Airport, he saw wildfires burning in the mountains west of the lake. To him it looked bad, but no evacuations or travel warnings had been issued yet. The routes leading north to Reno and east to Carson City remained unscathed from the wraths of fire and the Santa Ana winds, but that could change in a heartbeat. The smell of burning forests and the patches of low-lying smoke had Devin wondering if the devouring wolf in his vision could be fire. God knew swiftly moving wildfires had surprised and trapped a number of people already this year.

At the registration desk, he came face-to-face with a welcome sign and stopped in surprise. Along with a symposium on Psychiatry Today was a convention about Discovering the World of ESP.

He headed for the first available desk clerk. "Welcome to Les Moritz. Your name, sir?"

"Devin St. Claire. I don't have a reservation. Any room will do. Can you tell me if Dr. Caroline Ward picked up her messages yet? It's imperative I speak to her."

"I'm sorry, sir. With both conventions in full swing plus the summer crowd, we're completely booked. And I can't give out any personal information on our guest."

Devin's eye twitched. "I understand. I'd like to speak to your manager, please."

Thirty minutes later, he had a top-level suite and some reassurance about Caro. She'd picked up her messages this morning. The hotel management promised to deliver his note directly to her, so she'd either call or show up here. He hoped she'd come right up.

Sliding off his coat, he sank onto the couch. He hadn't slept on the way here but still didn't think he could. Not until he set eyes on her. He tried not to wonder where she'd been last night. It wasn't any of his business, but that didn't stop the squeeze in his gut. *Coward.*

The phone rang. Scrambling, he tripped over the coffee table lost in his periphery to get to the phone. Cursing his laziness for not memorizing his surroundings before relaxing, he answered. "Caro?"

"Devin. I spoke to Iris, she's fine, and nobody is dead. Why are you here?"

"I have to see you. To talk about something important."

"I don't want to see you, right now." She paused then whispered, "Not here."

Emotion hung heavy between them. They'd spent more time in their room than on the slopes.

"This is really important."

"More important than, 'This is getting old. Move on, Caro. I have?' I took your advice, Dev. I don't have time for this. I've a meeting for coffee."

He winced. When she called him late-night, last week, he'd spoken in desperation. He'd seen her a number of times for days in a row because of Iris's situation, and it nearly broke his resolve. Iris came home from the hospital and Devin couldn't shake his need for Caro that night. She called and he cut her off at hello. Childish and cowardly. "Look, I'm sorry that wasn't my finest moment. Don't hang up. Did Iris tell you anything? I have to see you."

"Just that."

"Where are you going?"

"Excuse me?"

"Caro, please."

"I'll be in the dining room downstairs. Maybe after I eat, I'll feel like a friendly chat." She hung up.

Shaking with relief, he threw cold water on his face, neatened his appearance and went downstairs. She might kill him afterward, but at least she'd be alive.

Crossing the dining room with a waitress, Devin saw Caro. He drank in her strong beauty—pert nose, determined chin, and milky skin. The blue of her jacket matched her eyes. He managed to sit at an adjacent table, excellently positioned to study the guy sitting opposite. Half-eaten cherry danishes and steaming coffee made Devin's empty stomach growl. After giving him a dead-eyed glare, she ignored him, dashing any hope she'd invite him to join them.

Devin immediately disliked the 'hair-sprayed-Botoxed-too-perfect' look about him. He had to be twenty years older than Caro and wore a goldmine around his neck and fingers. As he spoke, he tapped his finger on a book, resting on the tabletop. *From the Grave: Interviews with Serial Killers* by Dr. T.L. Shaw.

Devin's blood chilled. He couldn't believe it. He knew the premise of the book. Online, both real and fake psychics buzzed about Dr. Shaw's work. Devin thought the man had opened a gateway to hell and would pay dearly for it. Through seances, Dr. Shaw communicated with serial killers. He claimed his beyond-the-grave interviews would one day help society to stop killers before they killed.

"Dr. Ward. I'm glad you joined us last night. What did you think of the séance?

"Interesting."

"Were you surprised at what the Werewolf of Donner Lake had to say?"

"I read up on Wayne Arlan Wysman before the convention. Since he hung himself after his arrest, little is known about his childhood. Hearing his mother killed the family pet and served it for dinner sounded convincing as his first step into cannibalizing loved ones, then strangers."

"Then you see the value. Getting inside the monsters' heads is key to stopping the future development of them. Too many indicators are either ignored or fall through society's cracks. These men walked a pathway to becoming a killer long before they preyed on humanity. Will you join us tonight too?"

Devin agreed with the guy on killers leaving a trail before they kill, but no way in heaven or hell Caro would be calling on a serial killer again, especially the Werewolf of Donner Lake, given his vision. The man had tortured, killed, and cannibalized twelve women in the Donner Lake area.

"Maybe, I'll come. I'll text-uh-well, I'll leave a note at the front desk later today. I see the same system flaws with PTSD cases. My patients' problems start long before they reach a crisis, but I often don't see them until their worlds have fallen apart and serious harm to them or others has happened. Which is partly why I wanted to join you last night and meet with you this morning. I have a PTSD patient, but I think something else is going on with them. If you can communicate with the spirits of killers, is it possible for them to take over the mind of a living person?"

Had Devin not been sitting down, he would have fallen. Caro knew. Caro knew about Iris.

"Something like demon possession?" asked Dr. Shaw.

"Sort of. I'm still skeptical, but I have been doing a lot of research into psychic phenomena and there is too much unexplained not to consider it."

Shaw reached across the table and touched Caro's hand, and Devin fisted his.

"Dr. Ward, in my experience with the psychic world anything is possible. I'm a busy man, but I have to meet this patient. Set up an appointment and let me know the date. No matter what I'm doing, I'll fly into Atlanta the night before. We can have dinner and discuss the case in detail."

Caro slipped her hand from Dr. Shaw's. "I appreciate your interest and your offer. As of yet, I am not even sure possession is the situation. But I will keep consulting you in mind."

"Please do." Dr. Shaw patted his coat pocket and pulled out his cell phone then frowned. "This lack of service is damned annoying. I had a meeting with Dr. Robards this morning, but she failed to show. Have you seen her?"

"Michelle? No, not since last night at Donner Lake. She was with Dr. Carrington and Dr. Finds. Like you, they drove separately instead of taking the hotel shuttle with the rest of us."

"I'll check with them. Why don't you ride with me tonight, and I can explain more about the séances and my book? Truthfully, I'd hoped for a more passionate response than interesting. The more professional people supporting my study, the greater good it will do."

Caro smiled, and Devin bit his tongue to stop himself from answering no. Not because it would be rude, but if he did it, Caro would likely go with Shaw out of spite.

"I'll keep your offer in mind. I did mean to ask you the name of the Medium conducting the séance. She only introduced herself as Medici."

Dr. Shaw shook his head. "I'm sorry. Given the controversy in communicating with serial killers, I promised her anonymity. Thus, the name and her veil."

Devin slipped out his cell to text his Aunt Zena on what she knew about Dr. Shaw and Medici, then put it back with a silent curse. No service.

Caro's smile to Dr. Shaw didn't reach her eyes, leaving Devin with some questions and a breath of relief. She hadn't bought Dr. Shaw hook, line, and sinker. "I understand. Well, as I said. I will leave a message at the desk if I decide to attend. I really appreciate your time this morning."

"My pleasure." They both stood and shook hands. Dr. Shaw paused a brief second before releasing his grip. "I look forward to hearing from you."

Caro nodded then turned Devin's way as Dr. Shaw left. His gaze took in her long legs, blue skirt and lacy green top peeking from the neatly buttoned blazer—professional and hot—her expression cold and unwelcoming. "I am a more than reasonable woman, but at this point, you've crossed lines that—"

Devin rose and caught her shoulders. "You are in danger. Whatever coward or ass I am doesn't matter right now. You can deal with me afterward."

She frowned. "What danger?"

He sucked in air. The moment for truth had arrived, and he choked. "Let's sit." Releasing her, he glanced at the table and dining room filled with people. "Preferably someplace a little more private. If that's okay?" She shrugged, and he collected his cane.

Rather than insisting on navigating his way out as usual, he hooked his arm through hers. "Lead the way."

Arching a brow, she complied. As they passed the bar on the way out, Caro abruptly stopped and gasped. He turned to see breaking news on the big screen TV. *Mutilated woman's body discovered at Donner Lake. Caucasian, about 5'7" with dark hair, wearing a red scarf. If anyone has any information, please call the number on the screen.*

"We were just there," Caro whispered, her body shaking.

Devin shuddered he knew what death the woman suffered. And it could have been Caro. "Let's go." Free from obstacles, Devin used his cane to escort her to the elevator and up to his room. He sank into the couch and pulled her down with him. "The woman who is missing. What color hair does she have?"

"Who's missing?"

"The doctor who didn't show for her meeting with Shaw?"

"Dr. Robards?" Caro went ghost-white. "Michelle has black hair, and she… she had a red scarf tied to her purse. We have to call." After getting no answer from Michelle's hotel room, Caro contacted the authorities. She explained the séance at Donner Lake last night, and they asked her to stay close to the phone for a detective's call. After disconnecting, she stood staring at the phone in her hand. "I know Michelle. We went to college together."

Devin gently set the phone aside and eased Caro back to the couch. He cupped her cheek. "I'm sorry."

She set her hand on his, meeting his gaze. "You knew about this already? That's why you came. How?"

73

He exhaled. "I will tell you, but bear with me a moment. Iris is the patient you spoke to Shaw about, right?"

"You're her authorized representative. I tried to discuss this the other night, but—"

"I shut you down on hello. You have to understand; I can't be what you deserve. Your dream is a family, and my blindness is a genetic curse I won't pass on."

Grabbing his shirt, she narrowed her gaze. "I knew it. Damn it–" He pressed a finger to her lips, drinking in their soft warmth. His desire for her surpassed his strength. "Wait. There's more I have to tell you."

She gently bit his fingertip, and he groaned. "Well?" she asked.

"This is under Iris's doctor-patient privilege. No one can know and you can't let Eva know I told you. A spirit didn't possess Iris. Not really. Not yet. She's telepathic. So was my father. She tapped into a serial killer's mind during his kills and couldn't shut him out. Eva is an empath at crime scenes. And I, like my mother, have visions of the future. Never clear ones, but in allegory. Last night, I saw a massive wolf kill you on a moonless night. Tonight's the new moon. I had to get to you. Learning about Shaw's séance for the Werewolf of Donner Lake today makes my vision blood-chilling. Now a woman has died."

Caro drew in several deep breaths then asked, "How do you know it's me in your vision and not Michelle?"

He fanned his fingers through her long red hair. "You're unforgettable. It was you. I spent the last nine hours dying to see you, and I'm not letting you out of my limited sight until this monster is caught. I know this all sounds crazy but you have to believe me."

"I believe *in* you. I'll think about the rest." She touched the heavy cross he wore. "This is new."

"It's the St. Claire Cross. It's been in the family for generations. My grandfather was the last to wear it. Strangely enough, I found it atop your picture in my drawer." He paused as his brain fought to think clearly. "You know, I don't believe in coincidence. So maybe, this is why." He put the necklace on Caro.

She clasped the cross in her hand. "It's beautiful, solid and simple. You've never worn it before now?"

Devin shook his head. "As with a number of ancestors, he was a man of God who cast out demons and wore it for protection. After what happened with my parents, I don't know what I believe about God. So, wearing it didn't feel right. I do know I won't let anything get to you."

Smiling, Caro arched her brow. "Anything, Dev? You won't let anything get to me?" She leaned forward and kissed him, her warm lips igniting him, destroying any hope of being strong.

"Except for me," he whispered. Looking into her deep blue eyes, he drowned. "I... need you." He had to touch her once more, love her again. He returned her kiss hard, hungry for the taste of her. His tongue danced with hers, and his heart raced with want. *How could he love her and let her go again?*

He groaned in pain, in love, in need. "Ah, Caro." He shook as he caressed her back, drawing her closer to him. The feel of her lush breasts tight against his chest, burned. She slid her fingers into his hair, bringing him even closer to her as she met the demand of his tongue stroke for stroke. Insisting on more, urging him to take more, she straddled his lap, pressing against his aching erection. He gasped with pleasure, needing her more than he needed to breathe.

"Love me, Devin. Forget the world and just love me."

His blood roared in his ears, and his body shook from the height of his need. He barely registered the phone ringing or her escaping his arms to answer it. "I can do that," she said a few minutes into the conversation. "I'll meet you in the lobby."

Cold reality sent all the feel-good inside him crashing into his gut. He rolled to his feet from the couch and faced her.

She looked like a warrior goddess wearing the St. Claire Cross. He could see the battle in her eyes. Caro would never sit when she could fight. "What are you doing? Who are you meeting? We aren't leaving this room, Caro."

"It was the detective. He wants me to show him where we had the séance last night."

"Someone else can do it."

"We'll be with armed policemen in broad daylight. I have to go and do what I can for Michelle. None of it seems real to me. I keep thinking it's a mistake and she'll come knocking on the door at any moment. I have to go, Dev. You said your premonition happened at night. I promise we'll be back long before then."

"We both know life is never that simple."

Despite the hidden knife in his cane, Devin felt naked and

defenseless as they left the hotel with Detective Ryan. Seasoned and in great shape, the cop owned his badge and the gun holstered at his hip, but Devin couldn't relax. Especially when he saw how smoke from the wildfires had darkened the day.

"Are the wildfires spreading this way?" Devin asked as they headed to Donner Lake.

"Unfortunately, but with the winds down and rain in the forecast, things are looking better. What I'm more worried about is finding and stopping a copycat monster. Dr. Ward, I have to admit I was surprised to hear you and several other doctors were at Donner Lake last night. Until you spoke up, no one had called us. You want to explain what happened?"

Caro described in detail the night's events. "What did you mean by 'copycat monster'?" she asked.

"I don't believe in psychic anything, but since you went looking for the Werewolf of Lake Donner, I assume you're familiar with what he did to his victims?"

Caro nodded.

"Then you know what happened to this young woman. They're looking to see if it's Dr. Robards. I'll question everyone at the séance; you can count on it. Do you know of any reason why someone would kill her? Seems pretty convenient. You all supposedly dredge up a serial killer then one of you ends up dead using the killer's MO."

"I went to school with Michelle Robards. We'd fallen out of touch, but as far as I know, no one had reason to kill her. I didn't notice any undercurrents of animosity amongst the group last night or at any point since the convention started on Friday. Michelle herself seemed normal, cheerful, and talked about an upcoming trip to Europe."

"Was she going with anyone?"

"Kendra Jansen, her roommate in college. She lives in Florida."

Devin kept one ear on the conversation and both eyes on the diminishing light. The higher they climbed to Donner Lake, the thicker the smoke. Patches of it hung low over the road.

Suddenly, a woman appeared on the road directly ahead. "Watch out!" Devin yelled.

The detective slammed on brakes but still had to swerve. He tangled with the guardrail, leaving the front end hung up on the twisted metal. Everybody slammed against their seatbelts. "What the hell?"

Bloodied, barefoot, and in torn clothes, the dark-haired woman in the middle of the road stumbled toward them. The detective killed the now stranded car's engine and shoved his door open.

"Michelle?" Caro gasped. "Michelle!" she yelled louder, barreling after the detective.

"Wait!" Devin shouted, his skin crawling as a cloud of smoke blotted out the sun. Grabbing his cane, he had to fight his door open. Tree branches and bushes on the side of the road hemmed him in. He ran around the trunk to get to the road.

Detective Ryan reached the woman first. "Dr. Robards? Are you hurt?" He caught the stumbling woman's arm. She jerked upright, eyes feral with bloodlust. Blood covered her face and soaked her shirt. She stabbed the butcher knife she'd hidden into his gut. The only thing that saved the detective from the expert, disemboweling twist the woman gave the knife was his backward dive.

Caro stopped dead. "Michelle?"

Groaning in agony, the detective clutched his gut and grappled for his gun, then went still as if he fainted.

"Lock yourself in the car, Caro!" Devin screamed as the feral woman set her gaze on Caro. Devin waved his arms and shouted, drawing the woman's attention. "Here! Come this way!"

Snarling, the woman went right for Caro. Rather than going to the car, Caro ran for the woods.

"No!" Devin yelled, seeing his vision play out. He waved his arms at the woman again, running her way. "Here! Come after me!"

She ignored him, going after Caro, bloody knife held high.

Triggering the blade, Devin turned his cane into a spear and threw it after the woman, his soul daring it to pass through the very real killer. It pierced her back, jabbing like a giant needle into a voodoo doll. She didn't miss a step in her pursuit of Caro.

"Caroline!" Devin screamed. Pain bursting inside him. He picked up a rock and ran harder, but his limited vision hindered his speed. He couldn't afford to fall. Caro swung around. She looked at him then at the woman coming at her with a knife.

He threw the rock. It hit the woman's head but didn't stop her. She wasn't human.

"Michelle!" Caro yelled, then held up the St. Claire Cross. "Wayne Arlan Wysman, by all that is Holy, I cast you out of Michelle

Emily Robards and back into hell."

Just then a shot rang out. The woman collapsed to the ground and Caro, shock exploding on her face, clutched her chest and fell over backward. Turning, Devin saw the detective had regained consciousness and fired at the woman.

Agony nearly brought Devin to his knees as he fought his way to Caro. Reaching her, he fell to her side, thankful to see her frowning and breathing. Blood spread from a wound on her right shoulder.

"You're going to be okay," he whispered in relief. He tore off his shirt and belt and made a pressure dressing on her shoulder.

She struggled to sit up. "Who shot me?"

"The detective, aiming for the woman."

"Her name is Michelle." She tried to crawl forward to her unmoving friend. Devin's cane still sticking from her back. "Dear God. Please let her be alive."

Sighing, Devin went to Michelle. "She's breathing and has a pulse." He pulled his cane from her back. "Looks like she fell before the bullet reached her. Maybe you really cast a demon from her."

Caro held the St. Claire cross in her hands, then reverently pressed it close to her heart. "It saved her."

Taking Michelle's belt, he bunched her own shirt up to make a dressing for the wound and used his shoelaces to bind her hands behind her back before turning her over. She remained unconscious. Apart from the blood covering her, she appeared harmless now. "Rest here a minute. I need to see about the detective."

Whether she knew it or not, Michelle already had one death on her hands. Grim, he approached the detective, now unmoving on the road. Finding a pulse, and an extensive first aid kit in the car, Devin went to work. He just finished doing all he could when a Park Ranger came around the bend. When all was said and done, Devin knew Donner Lake's dark infamy would rise to a whole new level.

Two days later…

WOMAN POSSESSED BY CANNIBALISTIC DEMON AT DONNER LAKE—

Caro cut the TV. "This is Dr. Shaw's doing!" She paced angrily across the hospital room. "He didn't even have the guts to stay and talk to Michelle. The legal battle to free her will be a nightmare. And it's his fault. How can we convince a jury of that? Even I didn't believe it all until I saw it for myself."

Devin pulled Caro back to the hospital bed. "You need to rest now, or they won't let you out of here tomorrow. There'll be time enough for Dr. Shaw and Michelle's defense later."

She resisted and paced back across the floor. "Will there? What if he unleashes more of hell in the meantime? Who is going to stop him?"

"He won't be anytime soon. According to the police, his Medium has disappeared." Giving up on the bed, Devin pulled Caro into his lap. "Kiss me quick," he said.

"When did you get into my blues music?"

"When I didn't have you in my arms."

She sighed. "You know, we haven't solved anything yet. Being together won't fix the problem."

Devin's gut sank. He'd hoped to have a day or two more of heaven before walking back into his own hell of dying to hold, love, and see her one more time. "I know. I'm—"

She pressed a finger to his lips. "It's not because you've a genetic flaw. It's not because you've this psychic burden in your life. It's because you refuse to see any future beyond martyring yourself. I'll kiss you quick. I'll love you tender because I want you, I need you, I love you. Sometime, not tonight or tomorrow, but soon you will have to choose me over the demons in your mind."

She kissed him quick then kissed him hard, and he surrendered to his need of her. Right now, holding her and being with her was more important than anything else in the world.

6

THE SPIRIT OF LOVE

Bobbi Smith

Brett Jackson was excited as the stagecoach rolled into Virginia City. It had been a long hard trip from St. Joseph, but he knew it had been worth it. This was the beginning of a new and exciting life for him. He was a reporter, and he had come to Virginia City to explore the Wild West.

"We've finally made it," Robert Andrews said as he stared out the stage window at the passing buildings. Since the Comstock Lode had been discovered the city had grown.

"It hasn't been easy, but I'm glad we came," Karen, his wife, said. "It will be good to see Macie again."

Robert's widowed brother had died a few months before, and they were coming to visit his daughter, who had continued to run the family's general store after his death.

"Yes, it will."

"What about you, Brett? After making this trip, have you had any ideas of what to write about?" Over the long course of their journey she'd learned that the ruggedly handsome young man traveling with them was a newspaperman.

Brett smiled as he answered, "Well, I won't be writing about any Indian raids or stage robberies."

"I'm glad about that," she responded.

"So am I."

"We all are," one of the other two passengers agreed, knowing how dangerous it could sometimes be crossing the country this way.

It wasn't long before the stagecoach pulled to a stop in front of the stage office. The driver jumped down and opened the door for them. Robert got out first and then helped his wife descend.

Brett waited for the other two passengers to exit the stage before climbing down.

"Well, it was nice meeting you, Brett," Karen said. "I hope you find a lot of inspiration here in town."

"Thanks."

Brett was the last to get his luggage.

As the driver tossed his bag to him, he asked, "Where's a hotel?"

"Just a few blocks over," he directed.

Brett made his way to the hotel and registered.

"You staying in town long, Mr. Jackson?" the clerk asked.

"I'll be here a while," Brett answered.

"Well, welcome to Virginia City."

Brett went to his room and got cleaned up. A short time later he was on his way to get his first good hot meal in days.

"It is so good to see you," Macie Andrews told her aunt and uncle as they had dinner together at her home later that evening.

"We're glad to be here with you. How have you been doing?" Robert asked.

"It's been hard... Everything happened so fast... One moment Papa was fine and working hard, and the next..."

"I know. He was such a strong and vibrant man. When we got your letter, we were shocked," Karen said.

"What happened that night, Macie?"

"It was late, and he wanted to go back to the store and stock a few things. He said it wouldn't take very long, so when he didn't get back in an hour, I was a little worried and I went to check on him." She paused, remembering that terrible night. "That's when I found him–He'd fallen down the back steps into the cellar." Macie was quiet for a moment as she relived that horrifying moment. "He must have tripped over something. At first, I thought it might have been a robbery, but nothing was stolen."

Karen could see the pain in her niece's eyes. She got up and went to hug her. "You're one strong girl."

Macie appreciated their kindness.

They visited a while longer, and then Karen and Robert left to return to their hotel.

Macie was glad they had come to town, and she was looking forward to them moving into the house with her the following day.

Alone again, Macie grew restless, thinking about her father and how suddenly he'd been taken from her. It had broken her heart that she hadn't even had the chance to tell him goodbye. If only she'd gone with him that night, none of this would have happened. Sadness filled her as she wished she could have been there to prevent it. They'd been close, and Macie knew she would miss him always.

Although it was getting late, she was unable to sleep. She left the house and made her way to the store. Andrews' Emporium was his legacy, and she had vowed to herself that she was going to make him proud of her by keeping it open. She let herself in and locked the door behind her. After lighting a lamp, she went to the office at the back of the store to do some paperwork. Sometime later, she was hard at work at the desk when she heard it.

"Macie..."

The faint distant sound of someone calling her name surprised Macie. She couldn't imagine who would be out at this time of night. She went into the store, wondering if someone passing by had seen the light in the office and called to her from outside. Macie looked out the front window but saw no one. The street was deserted. Convinced she'd just imagined it, she went back to the office.

A short time later, she was really startled when heard it again.

"Macie..."

The call seemed to come from the alley this time. Taking the lamp with her, she set it on a table near the rear door and went out to see who was there.

And it was then that Macie saw it—the faint ghostly visage of her father hovering near the cellar steps where the accident had happened. Shocked by the vision, she froze, and when the ghost called out to her again, Macie cried out in fear.

Brett stopped at a saloon after having dinner. He got a whiskey at the bar and saw there was a poker game going on in the back. There was room at the table for another player, so he decided to see what kind of luck he was going to have in this new town.

"Mind if I join you?" Brett asked walking back to the table.

The three players looked up at him.

"Not at all. We'll be glad to take your money," one man told him with a smile. "I'm Jerry, he's Ken and the one with the pile of money over there is Hank."

"Good to meet you. My name's Brett." Brett sat down.

"Let's see your money, Brett," Ken said, his expression serious.

"Yeah, I'd like to see a lot of it," Hank added with a sly grin, ready to win all of this stranger's cash, too.

"Ante up," Jerry said once Brett had been seated.

Brett did just that and was soon caught up in the game. He'd never considered himself a good gambler, but he could usually hold his own. He won that hand and continued to play. One thing he prided himself on was knowing when to fold. The man named Hank was drinking heavily and raking in his winnings, leaving the other two men grumbling.

The next hand Brett was dealt was a bad one. He didn't even have a pair, so he folded early. As the others kept playing, the tension rose and the betting grew serious. Ken eventually dropped out, too, and Brett wasn't too surprised when Hank shoved his pile of money to the center of the table.

"I raise you this," Hank sneered with drunken confidence, "and I call you. Let's see what you got, Jerry."

Jerry's expression was calm as he shoved his money out to match him and said, "A royal flush." He spread his cards before him. "What do you have?"

Hank stared at the other man's cards in stunned silence, and then erupted in anger, throwing his hand with two pair on the table. "You cheatin', no good…" Furious, he stood up.

Jerry raked in his large pile of winnings, smiling. "I don't cheat, Hank. I just got lucky."

For a moment, Brett thought Hank might go for his gun. This was, after all, the Wild West. As is happened, though, Hank just turned and stalked out of the saloon, never looking back.

"Hank isn't the best gambler around town, and I'm real glad about that right now," Jerry said, proud of his winnings.

"I heard he's having some money problems," Ken added.

'I don't doubt it, and betting like that isn't going to help him any."

"He ain't the smartest man in town, that's for sure. Why the bank even turned him down for a loan."

"Where did you hear that?"

"I got my sources," Ken grinned.

"You good for another hand?" Jerry looked at Ken and Brett.

"Sure," Brett said as he anted up.

It was much later when Brett headed back to the hotel. He was surprised to find the streets were quiet. For all he'd heard about the mining town, he'd expected it to be rowdy and wild. Except for Hank's show of temper not much had happened so far, but then he realized it was mid-week. He had no doubt it would be a much livelier place come Friday night.

In an instant, the moment of peace Brett had been enjoying was shattered when he heard the sound of a woman's scream in the nearby alleyway. Brett drew his gun and ran toward the alley, expecting real trouble. He saw the back door of the building was standing open and a young woman was crouched down nearby, cowering against the wall. He moved forward slowly, cautiously looked around, but found no one else anywhere.

"What is it? What happened?" Brett called out to her as he went to her side.

"He was here. I saw him…" she whispered, lifting her gaze to the stranger standing over her. The man seemed like a guardian angel, appearing out of nowhere.

"Who was here? Who did you see?" Brett looked around again. The alley was completely deserted. He holstered his gun and knelt down beside her. "Did someone try to hurt you?"

"No… no… It was… my father…"

Brett frowned in the darkness. "If it was your father, why did you scream?"

Macie drew a shuddering as she tried to understand what had just happened to her. "My father's dead… "

"What?" He was confused as he took her arm to help her stand.

"Let's go inside," Macie said, feeling the need to get out of the darkness of the alley and back in the store where it was safe.

Brett accompanied her into the building. "Are you sure you're all right?"

"I think so…" She turned to face him then and realized she'd never seen this tall, handsome man in town before. "Who are you? What are you doing here?"

"My name's Brett Jackson. I just got in to town today. I was on my way back to the hotel and was just passing by the alley when I heard you scream." Brett looked around and realized they were in a store. The reporter in him put the facts together, and he turned to the slender, dark-haired beauty, asking, "Are you Macie Andrews?"

Macie was shocked. "How do you know who I am?"

"I came in on the stage with your aunt and uncle. They mentioned they were making the trip to visit you, and they said your father had owned the Emporium before his death."

"Oh, so you know Uncle Robert and Aunt Karen." She felt a little relieved by the news.

"Yes. Now, tell me, what happened in the alley?" Brett didn't believe in ghosts. He was finding the whole scenario troubling–and intriguing

"I know it sounds crazy," she paused, gathering her thoughts, "but I heard someone calling my name. I went to check out back and that's when I saw him... his ghost. He was right there in the alley when I came outside."

Brett was frowning, trying to imagine what had happened. Had someone disguised himself as a ghost to scare her? And if so, why? "And you didn't see anyone else around?"

"No, there was no one else. As soon as I screamed, he just vanished, and then you came," she finished, trying to make sense of it all. She looked up at him again. "Thank you."

"I'm just glad I was close enough to hear you."

"I am, too."

Brett realized there was nothing more they could do that night. "Do you want to lock things up and I'll see you home, Miss Andrews?"

Macie had always considered herself capable of handling any situation, but what had happened tonight had changed all that. "Please call me Macie, and, yes, it'll only take a moment, Mr. Jackson."

"I'm Brett," he returned.

A short time later, they reached her house. Brett made sure she was safely inside before he left her and once again started back to his hotel. He remembered then how just a short time before he'd thought the town was awfully quiet that night. Things did have a way of changing. He just couldn't help but wonder why she thought she'd seen her father's ghost. He knew he was going to have to do some investigating.

The following day Brett decided to stop by the Emporium and found Robert and Karen helping with the store.

"Brett, I'm so glad you came by." Karen went to speak with him the moment she saw him. There were customers nearby, so she kept her voice down. "Macie told us what happened last night. It was so frightening for her."

"That's why I came over. I wanted to make sure everything was all right this morning."

"Everything's fine. Thank you for helping her." Robert joined them.

"I was just glad I was there."

"She's in the office right now. Hank stopped by to see her."

"Hank?" Brett frowned slightly at hearing the name.

"Hank Wilson. You can go on back," Karen encouraged. She liked Brett a lot more than Hank.

Brett made his way toward the office, wondering if there was more than one Hank in town.

"I'll be looking forward to seeing you at the dance Saturday night," Hank said as he gazed hungrily down at Macie. He smiled to himself, knowing he couldn't wait until they were married and he could get her alone all the time.

"Yes, it will be nice. Now, I have to get back to the store," Macie told him, trying to move past him, but Hank blocked her way.

"Not yet." He pulled her to him.

"Hank, don't…" She twisted against his grip, wanting to free herself.

Brett heard her and immediately knocked on the partially closed door before pushing it open and walking in. "Macie? Your aunt and uncle told me you were back here."

Hank was irritated by the interruption. He let her go and turned, surprised to find it was Brett who'd walked in on them.

"Why, Brett, I didn't know you were coming by this morning," Macie was relieved, once again by his unexpected appearance.

"You know him?" Hank was surprised as he looked between them.

"Yes, we met last night when he came by the store," Macie answered him simply. She hadn't told Hank about what had happened in the alley. "How did you two meet?"

"I lost some money to Hank playing poker last night," Brett said wryly.

"And I'll be glad to take more any time you're ready," Hank told him. "I'll see you later, Macie."

Hank walked past them and exited the store, wondering what Brett was doing there. He didn't want any other man around Macie.

Brett waited until he was gone before asking Macie, "So everything's alright this morning? You didn't have any more trouble after I left you last night?"

"Everything's fine. And I've even got some extra help here at the store," she replied, smiling at her aunt who was standing nearby helping a customer.

"Looks like you got some good workers."

"That she does. Brett, maybe you could write an article on the excitement of working in a general store," Karen laughed as she moved off to wait on a customer. "Did you know Brett's a reporter?"

"You are?" She was intrigued.

"Yes, I came to Virginia City, to see what the Wild West was really like."

"I hope you find something more interesting than a general store to write about."

"I do, too. I heard Hank mention there was a dance coming up Saturday night. I'll look forward to seeing you there," he told her.

"I'll look forward to it, too," she agreed.

Satisfied that things were back to normal for Macie, Brett left the store and headed back to the hotel. He planned to stop by the newspaper office to see if they were hiring, and then he wanted to rent a room at a boarding house. He was going to be in Virginia City for a while, so he knew he should get settled in.

The rest of the week passed quickly for Brett. He was hired on at the newspaper and started working right away.

Macie was excited as she joined her aunt and uncle in the parlor on Saturday night, wearing a turquoise gown that fit her perfectly.

Karen smiled as Macie joined her and Robert in the parlor on Saturday evening. "We certainly picked the right dress for you to wear. You look lovely."

"Thank you."

"Yes, you do," her uncle agreed. "I'll bet all the men in town will be standing in line just to get a dance with you."

Macie laughed "Are you going to be first in line?"

Robert chuckled, "I am–if your aunt will let me."

"He will be," Karen assured her. "So we'd better get going. We don't want to be late."

Hank had been watching for Macie to arrive. He was more than ready for the night to come. Since she was done with her period of mourning, he was certain she'd be eager to marry him. He just had to find the right time to propose, and once she said "yes" everything was going to work out just fine. The moment he saw her come into the hall with her aunt and uncle, he made his way over to claim her.

"Good evening, Macie," Hank greeted her.

"Hello, Hank," she smiled up at him.

"Shall we dance?"

"I promised my first dance to Uncle Robert," she told him.

"I'm sure he won't mind, will you, Robert?" Hank looked to the other man as he possessively took hold of Macie's arm.

"Go on," Robert told them. "Have fun."

Macie found herself swept out onto the dance floor before she could say any more.

"I've been waiting all week for this," Hank said, smiling down at her. She looked downright gorgeous and he had no intention of letting her out of his sight all night.

"The dances are fun."

"Yes, they are, especially when I'm with you." He felt silent then, just enjoying having her in his arms. She was his and he was going to keep it that way. Yeah, once they were married he'd have her and the store, and all her money. Life was looking real good right now.

Brett enjoyed his new job, but he was frustrated when the boss asked him to stay late to work on an article for the paper. He finished as quickly as he could and then hurried over to the dance, looking forward to seeing Macie again. As he'd expected, the hall was crowded. He made his way in, keeping an eye out for her. He spotted her on the dance floor with Hank. Biding his time, he waited until the dance ended and then sought her out. Macie was standing with Hank and her aunt and uncle.

"Good evening," Brett greeted them.

"Why, Brett, it's good to see you," Macie said, smiling brightly up at him.

"It's good to see you, too." He'd always thought she was pretty, but tonight she looked downright gorgeous.

"It's about time you got here," Karen teased him. "I was wondering if you were ever going to show up tonight."

"I had to work late, but I finally got away."

"Good for you."

The music started up, and Brett wasted no time, turning to Macie. "May I have this dance?"

"Yes," she answered without hesitation, taking his hand and stepping with him out onto the dance floor.

Hank was not happy about it, but he knew there was nothing he could do right then.

Brett was glad it was a slow dance as he took her into his arms and held her close. They began to move about the floor in perfect rhythm.

Macie found she was thrilled to be in his arms. She looked up at him, to find him gazing down at her, his expression serious.

"You haven't had any more ghostly encounters this week?"

"Everything's been quiet."

"Good."

Not wanting to think about that night, she changed the subject. "What about you? Do you like your job?"

"Yes, except when I have to work late on the night of the dance."

"Well, you're here now, and that's all that matters."

"You're right about that."

They fell silent then, enjoying the moment. Though they were surrounded by other dancing couples, they felt as if they were alone.

Brett could tell when the dance was about to end, so he made sure they were on the far side of the dance floor away from Hank. When the music stopped, he led Macie to the refreshment table so they could get some punch.

There was something about Brett that bothered Hank, and as he'd watched them dance together, he knew he had to keep him away from Macie. He didn't want any competition for her affections. He'd just started in their direction when Karen spoke up.

"Hank..." Karen called. "I've been waiting all evening for the chance to dance with you..."

He was irritated but managed to smile at her. "Well, there's no need to wait any longer."

He took her out onto the dance floor, all the while wishing it was Macie in his arms.

"Would you like to go outside?" Brett asked as they finished their drinks. He wanted to get her away from the crowd and the noise for a while.

"I'd love to," she quickly agreed. She found she wanted to learn more about this man who had come into her life so unexpectedly.

They slipped away and found a place not too far from the hall They could still hear the festivities, but it was far more private.

"It's a beautiful night," Macie said as she gazed up at the starry sky.

"Yes, it is," he agreed.

She turned and smiled at him.

"But not as beautiful as you..." he said softly, as he drew her to him and kissed her.

It was a soft, gentle exchange, at first, and when Macie responded, he deepened it.

Macie was thrilled by his embrace. She'd kissed Hank a few times, but it had never been anything like this. When Brett suddenly let her go and stepped away, she was a bit confused.

"Why did you stop?" she asked in her innocence.

Brett slanted a wry grin at her as he nodded toward another couple that had just come outside. "I have to keep you safe."

She blushed. "You're good at that."

"I try my best."

"So tell me about yourself," Macie said. "All I know is you came here to write about the Wild West."

"You have made it wild for me," he told her, gazing down at her.

"I have?" Her breath caught in her throat as she saw the look in his eyes.

"Oh, yeah," Brett smiled, wanting to kiss her again, but knowing he had to control himself.

Teasing, she asked, "Are you going to write a column about

me?"

He laughed and took her by the hand. "We'd better get back to the dance"

"I know, I don't want Uncle to come looking for me."

Brett escorted her back inside, regretting that their moment alone had to end so soon.

* * *

Hank had been looking for Macie and when he saw her walk in with Brett, he grew even more angry. How dare she go outside in the dark with him? He knew he was going to have to let the other man know real soon that she was his.

"My dance, Macie?" Hank approached them.

She wanted to stay with Brett, but knowing she couldn't refuse him without making a scene, she accepted, "All right."

Brett stood back and watched as Hank led her out onto the dance floor.

Hank had hoped to escort Macie home, but it didn't happen with her aunt and uncle there. He was ready to propose, and he to find a way to be alone with her so he could do it. He headed for the saloon to get a drink and settled in at the bar.

"How'd your evening go, Hank?" the bartender asked as he served him his whiskey.

"Just fine," he answered, and he began to drink heavily.

"You still after Macie?"

"Oh, yeah. I'm going get her to the altar real soon," he told him with confidence.

"Well, I know some of the other boys around town would love to have her, too."

"She's mine."

The bartender saw anger flash in the other man's eyes, and he shut up. He knew what a mean drunk Hank could be, and he didn't want to rile him.

At the beginning of his trip, Brett had wondered if he was going to enjoy being out West, but now that he'd met Macie, he was glad he was there. She had made it all worthwhile. He planned to stop by the store in the next day or two and ask her out to dinner. He was definitely looking forward to spending more time with her. Deciding to get a drink before calling it a night, he made his way to the saloon.

Hank looked up from his empty glass just as Brett entered the bar. Brett was smiling and looking real confident as he came in, and Hank's anger ignited.

"What are you doing here?" Hank snarled.

"Getting a whiskey and maybe playing a little poker," Brett answered as he started to move past him.

Being reminded of the game where he'd lost big riled Hank even more, and he stepped in front of Brett, blocking his way. "Being from back East and all, you think you're real smart, don't you? Well, you ain't nothing in this town. This is my town, and you stay the hell away from my woman!"

The other people in the saloon backed away, knowing what was coming. They'd seen Hank like this before

But Brett didn't back down. He faced him squarely. "I didn't know Macie was your woman."

"Well, you do now!" Hank swung at him, hitting him hard.

Brett charged back at Hank, tackling him and taking him down. The two men fought on until the bartender came around the bar with his shotgun and broke it up.

"Get out of here, Hank!" he ordered.

Hank backed away and staggered toward the swinging doors. "This ain't over!" he shouted as he left the saloon.

The bartender looked at Brett and saw that he was rubbing his jaw. "You alright?"

"Yeah."

"How's a whiskey sound?"

"It sounds real good right now." Brett went to stand at the bar and accepted the drink the bartender handed him.

"Hank ain't no good. Never has been, never will be. I'd stay away from him if I were you."

"I'll take your advice," Brett agreed.

"Yeah, and him thinking Miss Macie is his," the bartender shook his head in disgust. "That woman would be better off marrying any of these boys in here over him." He gestured to all the cowboys drinking and gambling in the back. "Why, her father told me a while ago how he'd told Hank to leave his daughter alone."

"He did?" Brett was surprised, considering Macie was still seeing Hank.

"Yeah, she deserves better than him."

"What do I owe you for the drink?"

"This one's on the house," he told him, then chuckled, adding, "But don't tell the other boys. They might start fighting just to see if they could get one, too."

Brett was lost deep in thought as he finished his whiskey. The reporter in him felt he was onto something. Hank was having money problems and Macie's father had told him to stay away from her. He left the bar as soon as he was done.

It was later that week when Brett stopped by Macie's home for a visit.

"It's good to see you, Brett, but unfortunately, Macie's still at the store. She had to work late tonight," Robert told him.

"I'll go see if I can catch up with her there."

Brett was nearing the store when suddenly he heard a man's voice call out to him. "Brett..."

He looked around but didn't see anyone. He started on when he heard it again. He walked toward an alleyway nearby, expecting to find an old drunk, but what he found instead shocked him. The ghostly image of a man floated before him.

"Help her, Brett... She's in danger ..." the ghost whispered and then disappeared.

Brett was shocked. He took off for the store at a run.

"What do you mean, you won't marry me?" Hank raged at Macie. He'd managed to find her alone in the store, and thought it was the perfect time to propose. "I've been courting you for months."

Macie had been surprised when Hank had knocked on the locked store door that evening. She'd stayed on to finishing merchandising once the store had closed and her aunt and uncle had left. She hadn't known why Hank come, but after having dinner with Brett the evening before, she knew she was no longer interested in him.

"I'm sorry, Hank, but I don't love you," she said, deciding to be blunt with him.

Anger overwhelmed him, and he grabbed her violently by her shoulders, shaking her. "You're going to marry me!"

"Stop!" Macie fought hard to break free. "Get out of here!"

"I'm not going anywhere!"

Suddenly, the door crashed open.

Still holding onto Macie, Hank spun around, drawing his gun to face whoever had broken in. He found Brett standing there, gun in hand.

"Let Macie go!" Brett ordered.

"She just agreed to marry me," Hank said snidely, tightening his hold on her in a threatening way, as he whispered in her ear. "Don't say a word or he's dead."

"Somehow, I don't believe that," Brett countered.

"Get outtta here. She's mine."

"No, she's not." Brett wasn't about to back down.

Suddenly out of nowhere, the ghostly image of her father appeared, hovering before them.

"*Hank...*" Macie's father called out.

"YOU!" Hank shouted in horror. "YOU CAN'T BE HERE!"

"Papa!" Macie cried out.

The apparition floated closer to Hank.

Hank shoved Macie aside and started firing wildly in the direction of the ghost. "YOU'RE DEAD! I KILLED YOU!"

Brett was shocked by his words, and it was then that Brett made his move. He launched himself at Hank, knocking his gun from his hand, and taking him down to the floor.

Macie looked on, terrified as the two men fought.

Hank had killed her father?

How could he have done it? Why? She looked up at his ghost again as it stayed near her.

It was in that moment that the sheriff came running into the store, his gun drawn.

"Break it up!" he ordered, going after the two fighting men.

Brett landed a solid hit to Hank's jaw, knocking him out. He stood slowly and looked to Macie, holding out an arm to her.

Macie rushed to Brett, and he embraced her. They both watched as the sheriff dragged the staggering Hank to his feet.

"What's this all about?" the sheriff demanded, looking toward Macie. It was then he caught sight of the ghost of her father hovering near her. "Oh, my God…"

Hank was shaking in horror as he, too, faced the ghost of the man he'd murdered. "You're dead! I know you're dead!" he screamed. "I killed you! You can't be here…"

Stunned by all that had happened, the sheriff turned his gun on Hank. "You killed him?"

"He's dead…" Hank whined. "I know he's dead…"

"I'm taking you in for murder!"

At the lawman's words, the ghost vanished.

The sheriff wasn't sure what had just happened, but he knew that Macie's father's death had been no accident. He looked to where Brett was standing with Macie. "Are you two alright?"

"We are now," Brett told him.

"Brett…" Macie looked up at him as the sheriff dragged Hank from the store to lock him up. "How did you know to come here tonight?"

"Your father…"

"My father?"

"He appeared to me and told me you were in trouble."

"Oh, Papa…" Macie started to cry. "This is so terrible… to find out Hank killed him…"

Brett held her close. "I'm so sorry, Macie."

She gazed up at him, amazed by how he always seemed to show up when she was in danger. "I love you, Brett."

Brett bent to her and kissed her tenderly. "I love you, too."

In heaven, her mother and father smiled, knowing their daughter's wedding would be coming soon.

7

STRANGE DREAMS

Heather Graham

The First Night

The strange dream came to Piper Carrington on her first night in Reno.

She was by a small creek, and it was beautiful. Water, splashing and dancing with white tips as dazzling as diamonds over little rocks and rapids along the way.

The breeze was soft, and great trees held sway along the banks of the creek. Soft grasses grew on the banks, and the picture was ideal.

Then, she knew she wasn't alone, but, she also knew the man who set his hands on her shoulders. She turned to him, delighted, because she knew she loved him; he was her everything. They'd known one another since childhood, when their friendship had been fun, and mischievous, known him as they'd grown older, and everything in his heart and mind had touched hers...

Play had turned to flirting, flirting to a love as rich and deep as the years that had gone before.

He'd grown tall and strong, and the little cleft in his chin was still charming, while his jawline was strong and rugged. Dark eyes that had always sparkled with laughter now looked down upon her with love.

And then she was in his arms, and the dream became something more, something deeper; she could almost feel his kiss on her lips, and something deeper than beauty when they both laughed, and shed their clothing, letting it fall upon the soft grass of the river bank. They lay down upon the blanket they'd spread for their picnic, and it was the two of them in the strange wilderness that was now their home, the sweetness of sun and sky and the sweet-smelling creek, and the depth of the love that lay between them.

And then...

It was as if darkness and clouds blanketed the day. She sensed the danger and the horror, just as if the trees whispered a warning and the sun had dimmed in fear.

They were no longer alone...

There was a horrendous sound, and then...

A burst of red.

Blood red.

The Day

Piper awoke, gasping... and very nearly screaming aloud.

Somehow, she managed not to scream; she realized quickly enough that she was in her room in Reno, Nevada, there for Katie's wedding weekend, there—with her two brothers—for her parents' wedding anniversary. She glanced at the clock on the bedside table, and then flew out of bed. She didn't want to be late; Michael and Scott would torment her to no end.

In a way, few things had changed since childhood!

She dressed in jeans and a pullover and dug into her luggage for her boots. Today they were doing the ride out at the Montgomery Ranch, and—one thing she hoped to lord over either Michael or Scott—she did know how to ride. They might have all grown up in the city, but her summer job each year during college had brought her to Headley Farms, upstate as a camp counselor, and during her interview she'd sworn she knew how to ride. And so, of course, she'd learned quickly.

Hurrying downstairs, she found her family at a table in the breakfast room of the hotel and casino. Naturally, Michael and Scott were there ahead of her. Her dad and her brothers stood, always polite, but Scott already had that look in his eye—she was late, and she wasn't going to get away with it. She glared at him, warning him not to start. He shrugged, and she could see the laughter in his eyes.

She was a lucky girl, she knew. Her parents were great, like two wonderful Muppet-like people, born in the sixties, and simply bred to be kind and open-minded. Which had been good. Scott, their oldest, was gay, and now married to Aldo, who was so sweet they all loved him as they loved Scott. Sometimes more, Piper thought—because Aldo didn't like to torture her; he was fun and sweet and delighted to have her, since he had no siblings of his own. She remembered when Scott had come out to their parents and been stunned when his parents had been relieved. "We were so terrified you were going to tell us you had a devastating disease!" their mother had said. They were welcoming to Aldo and loved him like another son.

But, Aldo wasn't on this trip—neither was Genie, Michael's wife. They had decided this was going to be family, and their immediate family only. Piper even wondered if Aldo hadn't been the one to suggest the trip be this way—Piper had no significant other. Her budding relationship with Nathan Murton had ended in a five-car pile-up on I-95 last year. She had accepted what happened, but she'd always been slow to begin a relationship, and she was alone, and so…

Sibling time!

"Finally!" Scott teased. "Good thing we already ordered her coffee and a croissant!"

She made a face at him. Having two older brothers had often been a trial when she'd been young, but she adored them both—and thought they were extremely handsome men. The three of them were similar, she knew—her mother's dark red hair had come through on them all, and, conversely, her father's light green eyes. She stood a good five-ten, and her brothers, well over six feet.

"Now, now, be good to your baby sister," their mother, Katie, said. "We've plenty of time. We're not due at the horse ranch for another hour. "I'm so excited—but, of course, you do think they'll have a gentle horse for me, right? Piper is the rider, not me!"

"Mom, we don't have to go riding," Piper said.

"Are you kidding me?" Duncan, her dad, asked. He slipped an arm around his wife. "We have been looking forward to this!"

They really had ordered for her; in no time, she consumed her coffee and croissant, and they were ready to roll.

It took about twenty minutes to get out to the ranch. Michael, Katie, and Duncan went first to tell the guide about their abilities;

98

Piper was with Scott, a bit back from them.

She loved both her brothers deeply, as she did her folks. Scott, five years her senior, had often been her babysitter, and she wondered if they didn't have a bit of a special bond. He was grinning as he stood by her side.

"So, just why were you late?" he asked her.

"I overslept."

"So, just why did you oversleep?" he asked.

"Um, I don't know. Pressure at work?"

"Tour guides in New York are under pressure?"

"What are you getting at?"

He leaned low and whispered. "Well, you have this look about you... I call it 'the tousled look.' I'm desperately hoping that you got lucky last night."

"No, no!" she protested. "Oh, Scott, what are you thinking? That I just picked up a craps dealer and dragged him up to my room?"

"It would have been good for you if you had," he said, his look at her a bit sad. "Sweetie, you need someone. You're young—and I did see the way that craps dealer was looking at you! Carefully, of course—he wouldn't want to be fired."

Piper laughed and shook her head. "Hey, you always told me you were looking for what was right, and what was real. And you found Aldo. I'm looking for what's right and real, too."

She almost added, *And I found it in my dream. A dream so real...*

Of course, she would never say anything like that. He would analyze her. He would tell her she was so desperate and lonely that she was creating imaginary friends—or sex partners.

"We're up!" she said.

Scott led her forward, smiling at the young ranch hand who was helping to get them all mounted up. "Don't let this one fool you by trying to ride backwards or anything. She is the only talented rider in our group, so if we have a feisty horse on this outing, please—give it to her, and not me!"

The weathered man helping them grinned and assessed Piper and then Scott. "Well, I was going to give you the big buckskin there, Cheyenne. But, I'll be happy to switch around, sir, and give you Molly—the bay over there—and this young lady Cheyenne. He likes to bolt now and then—and eat the grass along the way. Not a kicker, not mean, just a prankster."

"Ooh, good, he's Piper's. Molly and I will be fine."

"Okay, folks," one of the ranch hands announced, "Yeah, we have some things in Nevada you need to watch out for in country like this—none you will encounter at the slot tables, but... once you're away from the neon lights, you never know. Black bear—probably won't encounter any, only about five hundred in the state. Mountain lions—there have been a few problems. Snakes—we got 'em, notably, rattlers. Scorpions... but, that said, you see anything, tell your guide. Don't panic, tell your guide. And, by the way, most of the time, our most dangerous situations have been traffic fatalities with cars and animals, including horses. Don't worry—you won't encounter any cars on our trails."

They started off along the trail; Cheyenne did try to eat the grass, but most horses would munch along the way if allowed to do so. Piper spoke softly to the horse and kept a gentle but firm hand on him. They were going to do fine.

The ranch hand was George, and he was going to be their trail guide, too. As he led them along the way, he talked about the settlement of the area, and how Reno had been named for a Union general who had been killed during the Civil War, and how, while settlers had been pushing the western boundaries of the states before they were states, it had been the discovery of gold and silver that had brought a real boon to the area. Montgomery Ranch had now been there forever, even though it had changed hands many times.

He was a good guide—giving them enough information to enjoy the ride without bogging them down in detail. As she listened to him, his voice gradually softened as if he were speaking through a tube, at a distance, or through water.

She was filled with the oddest sensation.

As if she'd been there before.

While Reno was basically desert country, the valley at the foot of the Sierra Madre Mountains offered a nice respite, filled with little creeks that allowed for the rich country they travelled now. It was suddenly as if...

As if she was back in her dream. The day was beautiful, the breeze soft, and the branches on the trees were just swaying to that gentle movement of air.

Then...

They were riding by a creek bed, and in her mind's eye, she could see a blanket spread out, and white rivulets of water jumped off rocks and boulders along the way, shimmering in the sky like diamonds.

They suddenly stopped, and Piper was jolted from her strange sense of déjà vu.

A man on a beautiful black quarter horse had loped up on the trail before them, like something out of the pages of a western novel. He was in a buckskin jacket and wearing a low-brimmed hat and sat the huge horse with perfect ease. Broad-shouldered, and when he dismounted, Piper could see he was tall, and truly might have stepped from the pages of a novel.

"Dan, hey!" she heard their guide saying, as she edged Cheyenne forward into the little clearing where they had stopped. "You're back. This is the Carrington family; we've got Duncan, Katie, Scott, Michael, and Piper. I was taking them on the creek trail. No cantering or loping with this group—Mom has only been on a horse once before, and Piper is the only rider in the crowd."

"How do you do," the newcomer, Dan, said. He lifted the brim of his hat, and for a moment, Piper's heart seemed to stop.

He hadn't stepped from the pages of a novel.

He had stepped out of her dream.

She tried very hard to smile and say "Hello" normally.

He had dark eyes set in a rugged, striking face, and...

A cleft in his chin.

"So, you're the rider in the group?" he asked politely, smiling, and looking at her questioningly.

"I'm not the best by any means, but I have ridden," she told him.

"First time in Reno?" he asked them all.

"First time," her mother said. "The children have joined my husband and me for our thirty-fifth wedding anniversary."

"Congratulations," Dan said. "Wonderful. I'm Dan Montgomery. This is my place. I'm so glad you've come out here—and that you're on my trail for your second experience with a horse. You have old Crystal there, and she is a doll. My dad bought her for me when I was ten, so she's a bit of an older girl now, and... George here knows I don't let just anyone ride her, but I'm willing to bet that Crystal loves you—horses have a great sense for people."

"She's lovely, so lovely!" Katie said happily. "The rest of us just feel badly that we're plodding along. I'm sure Piper would have preferred a more exciting ride, but…"

"Mom, it's your anniversary," Piper murmured. "I'm fine."

"I can take you to some grasslands where you can take Cheyenne for a bit of a canter or a gallop, if you'd like, Miss Carrington," he said.

"Oh, no, that's all right," Piper murmured.

Scott edged his horse closer to Piper's and looked at her with very mischievous eyes. "Piper, he can take you for a lope—or, a hell of a gallop."

She cast her brother an evil glare.

"Seriously, it would be my pleasure," Dan said.

"Go, please, go—make your mother happy," her father said.

"Dad, you always say 'make your mother happy' when you want me to do something!" Piper protested. "It's your anniversary—"

"Great—go and have a little fun as a 'happy' present to me!" her mom told her.

If she demurred anymore, she'd look ridiculous.

"Um, thank you," she told Dan.

Of course, her brothers were trying to throw her at the man—any man maybe, at this point.

"Come on!" Dan Montgomery said.

She wove Cheyenne through the other horses and came nearer to her new guide. The closer she came, the more she felt the strange sense of unease…

As if she knew him. And, of course, she didn't.

"This way," he told her.

She followed along behind him. He led his horse to a trot, and then, when they broke out onto an open field, a canter, and then—looking back at her to assure her comfort first—he broke into a gallop. Cheyenne, beneath her, moved with fluidity, and she thought, pure pleasure, almost as if she'd kicked up her heels to run.

It was always an amazing feeling, being atop a good horse, feeling the air rush by and the simple joy of movement. It was almost as if one could race the world away and reach some kind of a higher plane.

Eventually, they neared a new group of trees, and another trail led through them. He'd slowed his horse and, of course, she did the same, and Cheyenne automatically trotted up to ride alongside his great black quarter horse.

"Felt good, huh?"

"Wonderful," she admitted.

"Want to see one of my favorite places in the world?"

"Sure."

He led the way again, winding through to another break in the trees.

They were by a creek; water danced over stones. Little droplets were caught by the sun and seemed to shimmer as they fell like diamonds.

The breeze moved, sweet and clean.

And she had seen it before, the exact spot, just as she was certain she had seen the man.

He dismounted and walked his horse over to the creek. She did the same.

He turned to her. "I seriously think this is one of the most beautiful spots imaginable. I come here often; there's something magical about it."

She smiled uneasily. "It is beautiful," she murmured.

"So, where is your family from?" he asked.

"New York City," she told him.

"And you ride there often?"

"Not nearly often enough. I get to the park and ride when I can, and sometimes, I head back upstate to a camp where I worked through college," Piper said.

They stood by the crystal spring and allowed the horses a sip of water. He was watching her, curiously, she thought.

"You've never been here before—really?" he asked her.

"Never," she assured him.

He was still staring at her, as if he'd find an answer to an unspoken question in her face.

"I know this sounds... well, bad, I imagine. But, I could swear I've met you before."

Did people share dreams? When she thought of the rather erotic nature of her own, she felt a flush rising to her cheeks.

"Have you ever been to New York?" she asked him.

He nodded. "That's it—we passed one another in Macy's, or in the Village, or... somewhere! What do you do?"

103

"I'm a tour guide," she told him. And she shrugged, still flushing. "I love my city, and it's so rich, and people see plays and go shopping, but… there's so much more. Remnants of New Amsterdam, the Revolution… history of the country through the centuries."

"Maybe I was on one of your tours."

"I would have remembered that!" she said, and then, of course, she felt her face must have been blood red, because she had made it so obvious that she found him… memorable!

"So, what do you do?" she asked. Dumb. Obvious. He owned a horse ranch.

"Well, I lead the trail rides sometimes, but, George handles most of the ranch and we have some other hands who are terrific. I got out of the military and went back to school. Bit by bit," he said, and paused, looking a little sheepish. "Archeology. I've been on some amazing digs."

"Nice!" she said, surprised. She'd thought he was going to tell her he was a champion bull-rider, or something of the like. Which, of course, would have been fine, too, of course, it was just that what he was doing was… not what she had expected.

He grinned. "You haven't been on any digs lately, have you?" She laughed. "No."

He let out a soft sigh. "Well, I guess I'd better get you back to your family. Your folks—thirty-five years. Nice. Hard these days, but… everyone's dream, I guess. The forever kind of love."

She wanted to ask him if he'd found that for himself—no. She wanted to ask him if he was married, if he had a significant other, if…

If he'd been in a dream with her, a dream in which love was so real, it made every movement right and natural, and the act of making love into real magic, with diamonds dotting the sky, and the rush of the creek and the feel of the earth just an extension of two people.

She felt herself reddening again; the dream had just been far too…

Erotic.

And real. Just as he… had been real.

"Yes," she said briskly. "I should be getting back. I guess we've been a while."

He grinned. "The trail George is taking them on is a two-hour ride. We can catch up just at the end, race across the field, and take another trail—and we'll catch up."

She nodded and led Cheyenne from the creek, taking the reins and placing her hands on the pommel of the western saddle and the rear of it, ready to step into the stirrup.

He was quickly behind her, ready to give her a boost up. And then, of course, his hands were on her, and she felt as if she needed them there, needed them to stay there, to touch her more and more.

He must wonder why she was the reddest New Yorker known to man. His touch was totally appropriate; she was quickly seated in the saddle, and he was mounting his own huge quarter horse.

"Another race across the field?" he asked.

"You bet!"

They raced across the field again, and it was wonderful, slowed to canters, and then trots, and then walked. He led them toward a different trail, telling her it would lead them back through the trees— where they could catch up with her family.

Piper was a good rider—she really was. Not the best, but good.

Yet, just as they reached the opening to the trail, Cheyenne suddenly reared violently, again and again. Piper controlled the horse—just controlled him.

Dan quickly slipped from his own mount, catching Cheyenne by his bridle, and speaking soothing words to him. He looked up at Piper, frowning and disturbed. "I have no idea... he loves to run, but he's not skittish. I have no idea..."

"It's all right," Piper assured him. "Really—and I'm fine."

Cheyenne pawed the ground, obviously unhappy where he stood. Dan led him forward and paused a moment before remounting himself.

He looked at the ground there. Nothing but grass and dirt, near the shelter of the trees. He looked up at Piper and grinned then. "Hey, archeology. Maybe I'll try digging around here and find out if there is something beneath the ground, because..." He extended an arm to show that there was certainly nothing above the ground to spook the horse—nothing anywhere near them.

She had to smile back. She wished desperately that she'd never had erotic dreams about the man; she liked him. And, of course, he was attractive, and she wished she had met him on the streets of New York, or even through a dating service.

She still didn't know if he was even single!

"I would love to hear about it—if you do find something. Or if you don't."

"Make sure you give me your phone number, back at the ranch," he told her. "And, of course, you know, you can check with me any time. I'll give you my cell number. Right now, I'll get you back to mom and dad—and big brothers."

Yes, of course, big brothers were protective of their little sisters. Except for hers—they wanted her to have something going on.

They wanted her to be happy, she knew.

They met up with her family about ten minutes out of the ranch, and she told them that, yes, racing along with Dan had been terrific. They were all delighted for her, and very happy with their own experience at the Montgomery Ranch. Once they'd returned and dismounted and another hand had taken the horses away, they were invited in and offered water, coffee, or sodas, and snacks in the large, comfortable ranch office.

Dan Montgomery thanked them all for coming again and started out—then he returned to ask Piper for her cell phone number and gave her his own.

She saw the looks on her brothers' faces, and the sweetly naïve and oblivious looks on her parents' faces.

Dan Montgomery told them, "Cheyenne started rearing out there over something, and I'm going to try to find out what," he said.

"Oh, Piper, you were all right?" her mother asked, concerned.

"Mom, she can ride," Scott said.

"I was fine," Piper assured them. "Fine."

She wasn't really fine at all.

Dusk 'til Night Again

Soon, they left, and returned to the hotel, where they all went to their rooms to bathe and change for their meeting in the casino—the afternoon was going to be given over to a few hours of gambling the amount they had agreed they could lose.

"And, who knows?" Scott had said. "One of us could actually win!"

In her room, Piper sat on her bed. Then she jumped up, wondering if there was something *in* the room that had induced the strange dreams. She could find nothing. It was just a room.

She thought she'd indulge in a shower.

She showered quickly. The water reminded her of the creek and thinking of the creek reminded her of... the man, the dream man who had amazingly come to life in the form of Dan Montgomery.

She hurriedly left, heading down to join her family. She sat at a penny slot with her mother for a while, and then joined her brother, Michael, at the roulette wheel, her father for a few rounds of poker, and then Scott at the craps table.

While they were there, Scott casually talked. "We chatted with George—who seems to like the family. We're invited back anytime with a big discount. Oh, and he loves the guy he works for. Dan is not married, not engaged, and not—to the best of George's knowledge—seeing anyone at the moment. He was engaged before he went into the military, but they broke up with little acrimony when he came back—she'd apparently found solace while he was gone, and while he tried to be understanding, he just couldn't go through with marriage. Oh, and he rose to the rank of Chief Petty Officer in the Navy—pretty darned good for a non-career man and non-commissioned fellow. He doesn't even have a parking ticket on his record." He gazed at her and smiled. "Not to mention, he's gorgeous, decent as hell, and the kind who is interested in meeting your parents and family. Why do you run from him?"

"I'm not running from him—we went on a horse ride. He's not exactly running at me!"

"I think you run together. Mount up and ride into the sunset. Oh, my bad, double entendre there!"

"I'm going back to the slots!" she told Scott, pushing the few chips she had left into his pile.

Soon enough, it was time to head for the dinner her brother had planned at a sky-top restaurant, and she piled into the SUV Scott had rented to get them around.

When they arrived, they had a small private room that overlooked the neon of the city. The view was high and breathtaking.

A round table sat in the center of the little room. Piper noted there were six seats.

"We need to take out a chair," she said, starting to do so. "None of us wants to sit next to an empty chair."

"No, no, leave the chair," Adam said quickly, glancing over at Michael.

"Who's coming?" Piper asked.

"Oh, we asked the guy with the horses today," Michael said.

"George?" Piper asked, frowning.

"No, the guy who owns the place. Dan Montgomery," Adam said.

"No, no, no," Piper said, looking from her beaming parents to her brothers. "Seriously, you guys can't do this, please? I'm okay, really, I will date—just don't get mad at me if I'm as picky as all you. Mom, Dad, I want something like what you've had. I want to be celebrating my thirty-fifth wedding anniversary with my children, I…"

Her voice trailed. Dan Montgomery had arrived at the door to their little room.

She wished she could crawl beneath the table. Her brothers inviting him were one thing—her statement that she was just about asking for a marriage proposal was quite another.

But, she needn't have worried. Her brothers were immediately welcoming—bringing him in, talking horses, thanking him for coming. He glanced her way with a smile, a slight look of amusement, and replied to her brothers, apologizing for being late.

"Let me tell you why—it involves you," he told Piper.

"Me? How? What happened?" Piper said.

"Well, I told you, I have a compulsion to dig—archeology major, one more class to complete," Dan said, explaining to the family. "I called some friends and we went out to where Cheyenne was getting so feisty today. We started to dig—and found human remains. Old remains, down to bone and belt buckle and some jewelry. Anyway, experts are coming in—anthropologists and forensic types. I'll know soon, but it was interesting. They say that people do have an affinity with horses, or horses with people, or certain people. I think Cheyenne sensed something in Piper and knew something was there… and she wanted Piper to know. Sorry, I know some guys who would totally mock me for that—an animal is an animal—but, hey. Dogs are amazing—and so are horses. And people, of course."

"Since, yes, we're animals, too," Michael said. "Hey, let's sit. I'd love to hear more about whoever you dug up."

"Anniversary dinner—and we're going to talk about whoever was dug up?" Piper asked. "Let me stress the 'dinner' part of that."

"Oh, I think it's fascinating!" Katie said, glancing at Dan with a massive smile. "And so commendable!"

Their server came in. Piper's dad didn't drink, but Adam had ordered sparkling fruit cocktails, and they were served. If Dan Montgomery expected more, he didn't show it, and he seemed happy with their fixed menu, just saying how nice it was to be asked, and wonderful everything was proving to be.

Scott, Michael, and her parents kept the conversation moving smoothly, fascinated by his studies—and by the people he had out to his property.

"They worked so painstakingly, clearing the bones, and I was able to be involved. They know the skeletons belong to one man and one woman, and we're looking now to find out how they died—it's a different puzzle when you have bones—no soft tissue. There's a doctor from the college who is going to study the bones, and possibly find scratches or other breakage that would tell us more," Dan told them.

"All these years… and no one had any idea there were people buried there!" Katie said.

"And there are no urban legends that might suggest what happened?" Piper asked.

She was suddenly remembering the dream… not the good part, not even the erotic part.

She remembered the darkness, something falling over the couple.

Like…

A shadow of… evil.

He looked over at her and shrugged and then said apologetically, "I don't think I ever looked into tall tales and legends, though, as a child, you'd think I might have. I was into horses and G.I Joe, and I wanted to be G.I. Joe—finally turned into G.I. Joe—and knew there was nothing adventurous, exciting, or romantic about killing people and trying to stay alive. I'm sure that Reno—with the mining and the one time 'Wild West' element must have legends. I should try the library."

"Well, it's unlikely the two of them just died and buried themselves there," Scott said. "And, if it was a suicide pact of some kind… well, it's still not possible to bury yourself. I don't think."

"It will be something to look into," Michael said.

"I'd be happy to head to the library tomorrow!" Katie said, turning to her husband, "Wouldn't that be wonderful?"

"As you head into thirty-six years of marriage, looking for a legend about people being viciously killed will be great," Piper murmured.

Her dad was still looking at Dan Montgomery. "Absolutely, yes, fascinating." He looked at her mother. "I mean, we can't gamble all the time. We do have a few other plans, but I'd love to see what we can find. I mean, we were there—or almost there. Piper was there!"

"Yes," Dan said, looking at her curiously again. "We were there. I had the oddest moment, today, once George and I had discovered there were bones… we had just gotten friends out there, and when I was standing by the bones…"

"What?" Adam prodded.

Dan shrugged again, shaking his head. "This is going to sound really bizarre. I could almost picture a day, and yet, I knew none of the landscape had changed, and it was as if I could hear the water bubbling along in the creek, and the sunshine… and see them, as they might have been, right by the creek. Crazy, but… first off, of course, it would be natural if they were a couple, but… gunfighters usually killed one another. But, taking down a man and his wife— possibly murdering them in cold blood—I don't believe it was a common thing to happen."

"I've seen a few westerns," Piper's dad said knowingly. "Killers went and massacred whole families when a railroad might be coming through. '*Once Upon a Time in the Old West*,'" he added knowingly.

"That was a movie, Dad," Michael said.

"Movies reflect life—and death," Piper murmured. "But, of course—great movie, Dad, but it was a movie."

The cake Scott had ordered was brought in then, and the staff crowded in, all wishing Piper's parents the happiest anniversary ever.

Eventually, her mother yawned, and told her what a long day it had been. The party was breaking up, and when it did, Dan came over to Piper. "May I possibly drive you home—I'd like to speak with you."

The very sad thing was that it wasn't a pick-up line. He really wanted to talk to her about something that was bothering him.

But, Scott and Michael had heard him, and her parents, and Scott said, "Great—more room in the SUV. None of us is a little kid anymore, you know." He winked at Piper. She gave him a very fierce frown.

"Yeah, it's been the three kids in the back, just like old times,"

Michael agreed.

She knew she wanted to be with him, see more and more of him, but...

She also knew he was serious—he just really wanted to talk to her.

She smiled. "You guys aren't that big, but, of course, Dan, if you want to talk about something, sure."

They left the restaurant, waving to one another in the parking lot.

They headed to Dan's vehicle, a truck, but one with a nice cab section. He opened the door for her; helped her into the passenger seat, which sat high. She murmured a thank you.

And then he drove. For a moment, he was silent, and then he said.

"You're going to think I'm insane," he said.

"Try me."

"I thought... I thought I saw *you* at the site."

She frowned. "I—I was at the site. Remember? Cheyenne reared, and—"

"Not then, later. I had stepped back—the experts were in. And when I looked toward them and the big hole and the yellow tape... I saw you. Standing a bit back, looking terribly sad, and then looking straight at me, and lifting a hand toward me. And then, almost smiling."

She was silent.

"I'm sorry; I knew you'd think I was crazy. I won't bother you anymore; I'll drop you at the casino, and not bother you. Or your family."

"No!" she said quickly. Too quickly. But, words tumbled out of her.

"I could swear I've seen you, too—where you couldn't possibly be."

In my bed.

But, of course, she didn't tell him where.

"Really?" he asked her, his glance toward her a bit skeptical, but a half-grin twisting his lips.

"Yes, really," she said. She looked his way. "Very odd. It's as if I know you, and, of course, I don't know you, but, I feel..."

He nodded. "I know I sound as if I'm incapable of just asking you out. I am asking you out—if you don't mind, I'd love it if you

111

came out to the dig again. I mean, wow, you'd think I'd never been out on a date. I'd like to ask you to go out on a date, but would you think me entirely insane if I asked you back to the ranch for your first date? You're here with your family; they could come out, too, of course."

She smiled at that. "I'd be happy to come out, and it would be fine if they didn't come. I don't know if you've noticed or not, but my brothers apparently checked you out, and they're all but throwing us together."

He smiled. "That's great; you're lucky. My mom passed away when I was about ten. My dad, just a few years ago. No siblings. I have great friends, and I consider myself lucky to have them, but, you need to value your family."

"I do," she promised.

They were back at the casino. He insisted on walking her to the elevator, and then up to her room. He smiled slightly when they were there, and then he leaned forward, a question in his eyes.

She answered silently. He kissed her. He was real.

And then his lips parted from hers, and he backed away, as if he was very afraid he would do more, and it wouldn't be right.

"Tomorrow," he said huskily, and then he was gone, hurrying back down the hall for the elevator.

She could still feel his touch on her lips. And it was sweet.

That night, the strange dream came again. The creek, the dancing water droplets, the diamond-like glitter of the sun.

She felt him at her back.

And he was with her again.

* * *

Dan came to the casino to pick her up just as they were finishing breakfast.

She told her parents he had asked her to go back because he thought she'd be interested in the site; her mom and dad were great.

Scott and Michael were merciless.

But she remembered what he had told her, and she accepted their teasing. She was lucky—she had a wonderful family.

When she was back in the truck, she had a few difficult moments—she was sure if she were to see him—all of him—he would be exactly the same as the man in her very strange dreams.

But he was charming, and entertaining, telling her stories about the Navy, about friends, and the craziness of Nevada. And she quickly became enchanted by the man in the flesh, rather than the man who haunted her sleep.

At the ranch, George was heading out with another group, but he greeted her with a smile. "I have Cheyenne ready for you, and Jackson all set for Dan. If you need anything, Jill and Avery are working in the stable office!"

They both thanked him.

"Anyone out at the site?" Dan asked him.

"Not yet," George said, waving.

Dan helped Piper mount Cheyenne, then leapt easily atop his black quarter horse, Jackson, himself. Dan rode ahead, leading the way.

Things had changed since yesterday; a huge hole had been dug and cordoned off with numbers set here, there, and everywhere.

"They've taken the bones," Dan explained. "They're going to come out and continue with the site. Looking for... whatever they can find." He dismounted and helped her down as well.

She didn't need the help—up or down. She accepted it gracefully.

It meant that he touched her.

She stood by the site, at his side, and she waited...

They both waited in silence. She felt his hand slip around hers, and she squeezed his hand in return, and still...

Nothing.

"I am crazy," he said softly.

"Well, my mom and dad are going to the library. Maybe they'll find something out—I mean, something that explains who they might have been," Piper said.

He nodded. She paused, and then said, "Could we go to the creek?"

"The creek, my favorite place?" he asked her.

She nodded.

They remounted the horses and started to ride to the creek. As they did so, George and his group came out of another trail, and George called to Dan.

"Just give me a minute."

"I'll go on, if you don't mind," Piper said, arching a brow to him.

He nodded. "Of course, I'll be there soon."

He headed off to meet with George. Piper remembered the way, and Cheyenne brought her to the creek. She dismounted and walked to the water.

It still amazed her that it was identical as to what she had seen in her mind, in her sleep. She knew she'd never been there before, and yet...

Her cell phone trembled in her pocket and she answered it.

Scott was on the other end. "I found it, and you need to be careful around there. I mean, we're a hundred years later, but this is from a report to the sheriff's office, 1886. There was a party of ranchers rounding up stray cattle. They came upon a terrible scene. A couple mauled to death. They were Tina and Jared Gresham, a married couple who had just come to Nevada and purchased the land. The people who found them brought them to higher ground and buried them and reported the deaths to the sheriff—I guess they were all honest back then and you could just bury a body, or maybe... who knows. Okay, now, there are only—as George said— about five hundred black bears in the state now, but at the time... I don't know. Anyway, don't hang around any creek beds."

As he spoke, Piper heard something behind her. It was Cheyenne, bucking and rearing and trying to break free from the scraggly little tree Piper had tied the reins to.

"Scott, thank you, I'll call you right back—something is wrong with the horse."

She pocketed her phone and headed to Cheyenne, but the horse had reared high—and ripped the little tree right from the ground. The horse bucked again and galloped away at full speed, dragging the tree with her.

What the heck? Then, she saw it.

There were only five hundred black bears in the whole state. One of them had found her.

She stared at it; it stared at her.

Don't panic! George said. Tell your guide.

She didn't have a guide at the moment.

Then, the bear opened its mouth, and let out a sound that was terrifying. It stood up on its hind legs, and she knew it would fall back to all fours, and race at her.

She could run, but it would catch her. She could stand still... and it would

114

fall on her all the more quickly.

Run. She had to do something.

But then...

He came riding across the plain, racing at a full gallop, and he looked like a hero of old on his massive black quarter horse, almost as if he flew on an edge or pure air...

He seemed to move in slow motion at first, in a soft, strange mist of air, and she could only see him...

And pray he would come to her in time.

She had just met him.

She had known him forever.

He raced his horse straight to the water, and he swept her up as if she weighed nothing, and the fantastic quarter horse turned on a dime, the perfect quarter horse, and they raced back across the field, the bear in pursuit at first, and then...

The bear fell away, as if it had never been, and Piper was crushed within his arms as they rode, feeling the frantic beat of his heart and the rock-solid heat and force of his chest.

They rode straight to the ranch. He dismounted and drew her down, pulling her straight into his arms, holding her for an infinity. Then he drew away, and his lips crushed down on hers.

She barely knew him. She was madly in love with him, and she knew he loved her. It would be later... much later when they talked, and talked, and wondered if it was possible that they were the couple, somehow reborn, or if ghosts from the past had come back just to see they didn't suffer the same fate that two lovers had suffered before.

"Do you believe it could be, that we... that we are them, alive again?" Piper asked him.

And he told her. "I don't know. I don't know what I believe. But, I do know this. I love you, deeply, completely, and... I will love you forever.

One Year Later

She stood by the water, and it was beautiful. Dazzling little bits seemed to catch the light, and shimmer, as if they were diamonds.

The air was perfect, not hot, nor cold.

Then, she knew she wasn't alone, but she also knew the man who set his hands on her shoulders. She turned to him, delighted, because she knew she loved him; he was her everything. They'd

115

known one another forever, and everything in his heart and mind had touched hers…

He was tall and strong, and the little cleft in his chin was charming, while his jawline was squared and rugged. Dark eyes sparkled with laughter and now looked down upon her with love.

And then she was in his arms; she could almost feel his kiss on her lips, and something deeper than beauty when they both laughed, and shed their clothing, letting it fall upon the floor. She closed her eyes and heard the water and felt the breeze, and when she opened her eyes, she saw the Sierra Mountains rising majestically behind them.

Now, however, the Sierra Mountains were on the mural of their hotel room, and the water was in the giant Jacuzzi of the honeymoon suite they had taken for their anniversary.

A soft hum in the room was the air-conditioner, keeping the room at a perfect temperature.

Smiling, Dan lifted her, and set her into the Jacuzzi and joined her, and edged to her side, and kissed her, and said softly, "A dream, my love. You have made my life a dream."

She drew her arms around his neck and looked into his eyes for a long moment.

"Oh, no, Dan. Not a dream," she said, and as he started to frown, she quickly added, "Much, much better than a dream. So much better than a dream."

And then, of course, she kissed him again, and he kissed her…

And it was living in the reality of the most beautiful dream.

8

THE SECRET GARDEN

Lance Taubold

Bah humbug! Gray hated Christmas… no, he loathed Christmas. Scrooge looked like Pollyanna compared to him. His wife, on the other hand, had loved Christmas. More than anything. The entire holiday season made his beautiful Daisy shine brighter than the brightest star atop the largest Christmas tree. She embraced everything about the season: the giving, the food, the celebrating, the decorations…

Then she died. The day after Christmas. As she'd suffered those last few weeks, she swore she would live through Christmas, and at the last stroke of midnight, she'd died. Died, leaving him alone and empty. Five years now. And he'd had to endure five miserable Christmases without her.

They were both thirty when she'd died. Now he was thirty-five and *felt* a hundred and thirty-five. He looked in the mirror. There were small lines in—what Daisy had called—his handsomely rugged face. His hair was still a chocolate brown, like his eyes. He couldn't believe there weren't any streaks of gray in it after everything he'd been through. For five years he'd been a walking dead man. All life and desire to live had forsaken him. Why he hadn't ended it a while ago, he didn't know. He just wasn't the suicide type, he guessed. And Daisy would be so disappointed in him. Even in death, she still influenced him. He often found himself going to restaurants or stores, or places she'd loved to go to… just… remember. To feel her

117

presence, to recall the things she'd said and done at those places. Order food she especially loved. He wanted to stay connected to her. Not ever forget even the smallest thing.

Except for Christmas. For some reason, even though it was her favorite time of year, he couldn't do it. Maybe because, for him, she *was* Christmas. And that's when she'd left him.

Also the garden. Her "Secret Garden." Like in that children's book. It was her sanctuary. Her private world. All those plants and flowers—too many to count, multitudes of scents and colors. All of them had something to do with Christmas. Ironically, there wasn't a daisy among them, but they weren't a Christmas flower. And—she hated daisies. "They smell awful," she would say. "They're not like rosemary, which smells wonderful and grows in almost any climate. I mean, we're in Carson City—a desert! But these gorgeous plants thrive in it. Better than we do!" And she'd laughed. She laughed a lot. She saw the beauty and joy in everything—especially in him. She saw qualities in him that he didn't realize he had. She'd brought them out in him.

Where were these qualities now? Dead. Just like the plants in her garden. He'd let them die. Well, to be frank, oddly, he hadn't let them die. They'd seemed to do it all on their own. Like *they'd* lost the will to live.

Like he had.

But not entirely. He was still here, but a shell of who he once was.

He'd gone to her garden twice. The first was the day after he'd buried her. He'd hoped... he didn't know what he'd hoped. But the garden was a bleak and barren as his heart. Granted, it was December and most of the flowers didn't bloom then, but somehow he thought there would be something. The Christmas cacti were always covered with blooms—nothing. Not one bud. Rosemary—brown. It was as if there hadn't been life there in years. As if... only *she* could give it life. Like she had to him.

The second time he'd visited had been that following spring, March 21, the first day of spring—and her birthday. He'd expected to see the beginnings of life, buds, greenery...

But he'd been wrong.

There was not one blossom or bud anywhere. It was as moribund as when he'd been there in December.

The garden was dead.

His Daisy was dead.

He wished he were dead.

Their home in the southeastern part of Carson Valley was just minutes from Carson City. Great hiking. Four-wheeling. He and Daisy had done so much together. Their home was modest-sized, on half an acre, open. The area around them was sparsely populated, a few neighbors (within a mile or so) but not too many.

At the end of the back of the property was an eight-foot-high wooden structure, stretching back forty feet or so and almost a hundred feet wide. Within it: The Secret Garden. Her Secret Garden.

Now a cemetery of Christmas plants.

He stood outside the gate to the garden, wondering if he should have one more look. Maybe there was some breath of life left in there. This whole area, Carson City, Virginia City, Reno was purportedly the most haunted region in America. Perhaps some spirit could breathe life back into her garden.

He thought about their excursions to the Washoe Club with the Millionaire's Club/brothel, the Bucket of Blood, the Red Dog Saloon. All their favorite haunts—literally, some of the most haunted places in the area. Daisy had sworn several times that she could feel the ghosts, and a couple of times had seen apparitions of a saloon girl and a soldier. She had believed in the supernatural, and he had gone along with it because of her. Personally, the jury was still out for him. He wasn't convinced of the paranormal and such. He thought that if it were true then his Daisy would have appeared to him by now.

And she hadn't.

He reached for the lock on the gate to the garden.

"Excuse me."

Gray yelled, "What the—"

"I'm sorry. I didn't mean to startle you."

He turned and looked into the greenest eyes he'd ever seen. They shone like brilliant emeralds in the afternoon light. The eyes were set into a doll-like face, surrounded by ebony hair, cut short with jagged points at the sides and on her forehead. The effect was stunning. She was short, maybe five-two or three, but had a commanding presence despite her stature.

He stared.

She smiled.

119

He froze.

That smile.

Devastating.

Perfect white teeth in a perfect mouth with lush lips, tinted red.

She said, "Hi, my name's Jasmine—Jazz. I think I'm lost. I saw your house and there aren't that many around. I just moved a couple of months ago from Seattle and this is my first Christmas here and I wanted to get a tree—not a big one—but something so I don't feel so alone, being it's my first time away from Seattle. I've lived there my whole life, not that I'm *that* old. I'm thirty-two, as of March twenty-first..."

Gray's jaw dropped.

March twenty-first: Daisy's birthday.

"I'm sorry, did I say something wrong? You look like you just saw a ghost—"

"No," he broke in, "It's all right. I remembered something I need to do later. Please, go on."

"Oh, if you need to go, that's OK. I just need to know where the tree place is. A man told me it was on Six Mile Canyon Road."

"Yep, the Platt place. Amber runs it now after her folks passed away a few years back. You're not too far away. You should have turned left at the last intersection—the only intersection. Then it's a mile or so down. Nice girl, Amber, good talker."

"Oh good, great! Thank you..." She offered her hand.

"Sorry, I didn't mean to be rude. Gray. It's Gray." He took her proffered hand and squeezed it. He felt a rush of warmth when their hands met, in spite of the chill in the air.

"Oh!" Jazz said, quickly withdrawing her hand. "Yours is hot."

"I... I..." Gray was flustered, something he was not used to. "I thought it was your hand."

Jazz reached tentatively for his hand and took it in her own.

Her hand was cool now when she grasped it.

"How strange," she said. "I wonder how that hap—" She looked up into his eyes.

They stared at one another, Gray's hand held in her two.

"Ahem," he muttered.

"Oh, sorry." She released her grip. "You have nice hands. Strong."

He quirked a smile at her statement. "And yours are soft." Was he flirting? No. It was a natural response, he told himself. And her hands *were* warm and soft.

Jazz smiled a little awkwardly and mumbled, "Thank you." She looked up and past him, abruptly changing the mood. "What's this?" She pointed to the door, the Garden door he was contemplating opening.

"A garden," he said tersely.

She pulled back at his demeanor switch. "Oh. What kind of garden?" she ventured.

Gray realized his rudeness and softened his response. "A Christmas garden. Well, it was, anyway. But the plants have all died. I was..." What was he about to do?

"Oh, that's a shame. I *love* Christmas plants. Most of them are usually hardy. Maybe they're dormant. May I see them?"

What could he say? He'd already been rude. He couldn't let her see Daisy's garden. It was hers. And it was dead. There was no life left.

He pulled the key from his jacket pocket and inserted it in the padlock. What was he doing? Why was he doing this? This woman— Jazz—was a stranger. No one.

He removed the lock and flipped back the hasp. He put the lock in his pocket along with the key. He pulled the door back and Jazz brushed by him and walked in.

She gasped.

Gray followed her in and looked where she did.

Rotted, decayed, brown plants covered the expanse from wall to wall. The sun shone brightly on them, highlighting the bleak devastation.

"How sad." Jazz looked up at him and he saw tears in her eyes. She turned and slowly made her way through the garden.

He watched her walk, noting the way she would touch the various plants Daisy had loved so much, but he, curiously, didn't mind as he'd thought he would.

He didn't follow her but let her wander. He could hear her mumble occasionally the names of each of the plants. "Rosemary. Amaryllis. Poinsettias. Holly..."

"Gray, look!" The excitement in her voice made him rush to her.

"Are you all right?"

She was kneeling by a brown, scraggly, bushy-looking thing.

"It's alive." She moved back a little and gently raised a small piece of scraggle. It was… green!

"It's rosemary, for remembrance. Isn't it beautiful?"

While it was only the smallest of tendrils, it was indeed… beautiful. Gray nodded, speechless. How?

"Maybe it's not hopeless after all," Jazz said cheerily, oblivious to Gray's silence and bafflement. "I should be going." She rose and found herself almost nose to nose with Gray. "Sorry, I…"

Gray snapped out of his daze. "Wha… It's fine. I shouldn't have… I'll walk you to your car."

She walked through the gate and he locked it behind them. He turned to follow her as she walked away, now noticing her perfectly fitting, tight, white jeans, how they conformed to her perfectly tight buttocks and long-muscled legs. She was incredibly sexy.

She turned around quickly, as if sensing his assessment of her backside. "Coming?"

He was caught and felt himself redden.

Jazz smiled sweetly, but seductively.

She *did* know he was staring at her butt! *Shit.* He was a pig. Just another immature, drooling pig of a man… But he wasn't. That wasn't him. He'd *never* been like that. He respected women and hated men that… did what he'd just done!

Double shit.

"Jazz, I—"

She held up a hand to cut him off. "I think you're very sweet to have taken the time to show me your garden. You've been very gracious and kind. I'm sure you have better things to do than talk to some crazy woman who can't follow directions. Thank you again."

Who was gracious? She was. She'd bailed him out of that awkward spot with the briefest aplomb. "You're welcome," he said. *Maybe I should ask her to dinner.*

"Dinner? Uh, sure," she said. "When? Tonight?"

I guess I said it out loud. "OK." Who was saying this? He hadn't asked anyone out since he'd dated Daisy. Now here he was.

"I'll meet you here, if that's OK… since I know where it is. Seven?"

"OK." Since when had his vocabulary dropped to two letters? She waved at him and got in her car. "See you then."

His hand rose in response.

Oh God.

* * *

"I thought we'd barhop, if that's OK with you," Gray said from behind the wheel of his red, 4x4 Dodge Ram.

"Sounds great. I really don't know anywhere around here. I usually go into Reno. Everything's close there. It's easier. The casinos, you know…"

"I do. I don't go there much. Or much anywhere. I like the real local feel. We don't have many bars, but they're good ones. Lots of color and history. People know one another."

"I heard some of them are haunted. Your friend, Amber Platt—and thank you for that, I got a beautiful little tree from her, and she was just delightful—told me quite a bit about all the haunted places."

"Haunted? In this area *everything* is haunted."

"Really? I've always been fascinated by the paranormal."

Gray gave her a sidelong glance. "My wife—" He bit his tongue.

"Oh!" Jazz squealed. "I'm *so* sorry. I didn't know you were married. I would *never*… I just assumed—"

"She died."

Jazz was silent. After a few seconds, she said. "Now, I'm truly sorry. I… How long ago?"

"Five years. This month. Cancer."

"It must be hard. Especially around the holidays."

"It is, but…" Gray took a deep breath, debating what to say. He plunged in. "It was her favorite time of year, Christmas. She was a *freak* for it. The garden, her Secret Garden—she loved that stupid book—and the musical. We had to go wherever it was playing: New York, L.A., that summer theater in Utah that I can never remember the name of. Anyway, that's why the garden has all Christmas plants. From all over the world. I don't know much about them. She tried to tell me. In one ear and out the other. Sometimes I wish I'd paid more attention. Then… I don't know. I've never talked about it."

She placed her hand on his forearm. "Thank you, Gray. Thank you for telling me, and…"

She withdrew her hand from his arm and Gary felt the spot where it had been grow cold. Odd.

"And," she continued, "since it looks like there might be some life left in the garden, I would be happy to try and bring it back.

Modestly, I say, I'm somewhat of an expert as well on Christmas plants."

Gray thought for a moment. Decided. "Why not? You couldn't exactly hurt anything." He looked at her. She gave a soft smile in return.

She broke the moment. "So where are we going?"

"We're there." He stopped the truck. In front of them, crammed between two other buildings, was a semi-dilapidated, four-story, red-brick building. A wooden staircase led up to the porch at the entrance. There were arched windows in rows up the length of the four stories. On the second-floor balcony stretched a sign in blue letters on a white background: Silver Dollar Saloon.

"Well, it's creepy enough to be haunted," Jazz declared. "How fun!"

"This is the best place on Fridays—which it is. Have you ever had a horseradish Bloody Mary?"

Jazz shook her head.

"They're amazing. Ralph makes the best." He got out of the truck and went around to her side to help her out.

She took his hand and he helped her down. "This is a little high for me. Not everyone is six feet tall."

He grinned.

"We're going to eat too, right?" she asked.

"Oh sure. I thought we'd stop here, then grab a pizza at the Red Dog. It's just down the street. Oh, I'm sorry, I'm just assuming..." He could've kicked himself. "I asked you to dinner. Pizza and barhopping is not exactly a sit-down steak dinner. I apologize. I'm not good at... at this dating thing. I guess that's what this is. Shit! I need to shut up."

Jazz was laughing. "Don't beat yourself up, Gray. I'm having fun. And, truth be told, this date is already way better than the last couple I've had—which, if I recall, was over a year ago. Come on, my mouth is watering for a horseradish Bloody Mary." She grabbed his hand and they went inside.

The bar was crowded, and all the stools the length of the bar were filled.

"Wow," Jazz uttered. "This is so... awesome!"

"Glad you like it—" Gray broke off, grabbed her arm and dragged her to a corner table, where a couple was standing to leave.

"Perfect timing. You sit. I'll get the drinks."

Waiting for the drinks, Gray kept stealing glances at Jazz while she marveled at the decor and the locals in the bar. He saw her smile at the suspended clothesline, adorned with oversize bras and various other lingerie. She had a great smile.

He picked up the drinks and turned to see a bearded man in a full Confederate uniform sitting down across from Jazz. Gray grinned. Chauncey was local color personified. He had more stories than O. Henry. Especially ghost stories. He wondered what time Red Dog closed on Fridays. When Chauncey got into his raconteur mode, it could be an all-nighter.

"Thank you, Gray," Jazz said, taking her celery-decorated drink from him. "Chauncey here says he knows *all* the stories about ghosts and hauntings in the area."

"Yes, he does."

"Yes, I do."

Gray and Chauncey said at the same time.

"I have your chair, young man," Chauncey said, but made no move to get up.

"That's all right, Chauncey. I'll stand here next to Jazz."

Without acknowledging Gray's largesse, Chauncey continued, "As I was saying, *every* bar in Virginia City is haunted and has its own history. Now, I don't how much time you young folks have got—"

"We were only going to grab a quick one, then head to the Red Dog for pizza. Jazz is new in to—"

"Ah, the Red Dog Saloon…"

Gray noticed Chauncey's twang get thicker.

Chauncey adjusted his Rebel cap, scooted his chair closer to the table, gave a long wink to Jazz, and began. "In summer of 1965, Chandler A. Laughlin III—you probably know him as Travus T. Hipp, the radio pioneer and news commentator—started, what he called the Red Dog Experience. He combined traditional folk music and the newly emerging psychedelic rock scene. There was no distinction between the performer and the audience. He created a new sense of community. Of course, a little Indian peyote might have helped them enhance their experience." He chuckled and coughed a little. Gray and Jazz laughed with him.

"The Red Dog started the careers of some of the biggest groups of the day, like the Charlatans, and Big Brother and the Holding

Company, *wiiith…*" He paused for dramatic effect. "None other than… Miss Janis Joplin! That's right." He let that settle into their brains. "It's a different place all right. You'll see what I mean, Miss Jazz."

"I can't wait," Jazz replied enthusiastically. "And Gray, you were right. These Bloody Marys are *delicious*. But potent," she added. "Chauncey, I could listen to you all night, and next time I will, but I really do need to eat something or you and Gray will have to carry me home."

Gray found himself warming to the thought of holding her. Her white sweater clung to her very becomingly, and several times he had to stop his hand from lingering longer when he touched her. The evening wasn't too cold—especially for December. He had also worn a warm sweater and had brought a watch cap just in case it got colder. His plan had been to not be outside too much, and the bars around town were all fairly close together. So not too much walking outside. Of course, they could always drive, but Gray liked to stroll the quaint streets of the town.

"Red Dog, eh?" Chauncey started up again. "Make sure you get the Tommyknocker, Gray. She'll love it."

"That was the plan, my friend," Gray said, putting a hand on Jazz's back and helping her up, wanting to knead the soft fabric of her sweater… and what was under it as well. He knew he needed to quell his thoughts. His re-found desire was disconcerting.

Jazz looked up into his eyes. "Tommyknocker? Like Stephen King?"

Gray laughed. "No, it's an incredible veggie pizza they serve. Dee-licious. And this coming from a tried-and-true carnivore."

"So, the savage beast is a meat-lover?" Jazz smiled coyly. "Me too."

"Good to know," he said. "And the only scary about the Tommyknocker is how much you'll eat!"

"Can't wait. I'm starved. Bye, Chauncey. See you soon, I hope."

"I hope so too, young lady. Take good care of her, Gray. She's a keeper."

"I will, Chauncey. Thanks for the stories," Gray said.

As it turned out, the Red Dog was also known for its Bloody Marys, and they sampled another two of their famous drinks. And three-quarters of a Tommyknocker later, Gray and Jazz declared they had reached their limit.

"Would you like another drink or dessert?" Gray asked.

"Are you kidding? I'm going to have to work out every day for the next month!" Jazz exclaimed, then added, "But it was worth it." She patted her stomach. "We can't all be naturally muscular and trim like you. Some of us have to work at it."

Gray laughed, but felt a flutter of flattery knowing she liked the way he looked. He also noted how much he had been laughing this evening. It had been a long time. Not since... He closed his mind. "Would you like a doggie bag?"

"Most definitely. Cold pizza in the morning? The best." She started to laugh. Then laughed some more. She tried to speak but couldn't form the words. "Is... is it..."

Her laughter was infectious. Gray found himself joining her. "What? What is it?"

She struggled. "Is it... a... *Red... Doggie...* bag?" She let a loud and explosive laugh as she said it.

Gray guffawed as well.

After several moments, they wiped away their tears, noticing several customers around them staring. "I think we caused a scene," Jazz said, sniffling. "Sorry."

"I wouldn't worry too much. This place has seen a lot worse than a couple of tipsy lunatics having a few laughs. And... and by *God*, it feels good to laugh."

"Yes, it does. Laugher is healing. It's good for the soul."

Gray reached out and took her hand, and in his most serious voice said, "Thank you, Jazz. Thank you."

Jazz's eyes sparkled. "You're welcome."

"Last call!" the bartender yelled.

"Is it that late?" Jazz asked.

"Yep. Almost nine," Gray said.

"Nine?"

"I know, kind of crazy, but that's a small town for you."

"Well, it's been a wonderful—if short—evening," Jazz said.

"Yeah, it has been. We'll have to do it again." Gray realized how much he wanted to see her again.

"I'd like that," she responded. "And if it would be all right, I meant what I said about your garden. I'd really like to try to bring it back. Would Sunday be OK?"

Gray saw the look of hope in her eyes, and automatically answered, "Sure. Sunday is fine." He thought for a moment. *Why not?* "If you come early, we could go to the Washoe Club in the after—"

"The Washoe Club? That's the Millionaire's Club! I saw it on *Ghost...* or *Spooky...* something. One of those ghost-hunter shows. It was fascinating. I'd *love* to."

Gray grinned at her. "It also has a saloon in it. And sometimes some pretty good bands. But I haven't been for a long time."

"Is nine too early?" she asked, the excitement evident in her voice.

"That's fine."

"I can't wait. I need to brush up on my haunted lore in this area. Maybe tonight I'll get on the Internet. Of course, every time I do that, I get lost for hours. Oh well, it's the weekend. Shall we?" she took his arm.

He gave her a smile. "Sure."

* * *

Gray spent Saturday thinking about Sunday, and at one point found himself, late in the afternoon, in the Secret Garden, standing in front of a dried, brittle, brown rose bush.

His rose bush. Daisy's dying, unfulfilled wish.

Lying on her bed in the hospital, Gray recalled her words: "If only I could have created that rose for you, my love: the Gray Rose. My only regret. I wanted it so much for you. Then I could go. But things don't always go as planned, do they?" She'd given him a wry smile while the tears streamed down his face, and he'd clutched her hand hard in his. She'd closed her eyes, then, and Gray thought she was gone.

Then, abruptly, she'd opened her eyes and said, "You have made me so happy. I'll always be with you."

And for the final time, she'd closed her eyes.

That *goddamned* rose. Why couldn't it have bloomed? It was all she wanted. She'd tried for years, cutting, grafting. It was an obsession. She'd gotten close—a purplish silver—but never gray.

"Why couldn't you give her this one thing?" he yelled to the sky. He felt cool dampness on his cheeks. He wiped his face. "Fucking Christmas," he muttered.

A thought struck him. He went over to the plant where Jazz had seen the speck of green on the—what was it?—rosemary. Yeah, rosemary... for remembrance, Jazz had said. He bent down and looked.

Green.

And more than a speck. It looked like *several* little leaves were green. How?

"Are you here, Daisy? Is this some kind of sign? What're you trying to tell me? Remembrance? Remember you? Remember what? Help me. *Tell* me."

Silence.

A slight breeze.

He put his hands in his jacket pockets as he stood up.

He felt different somehow. Something had changed. Not just the plant. In him.

He glanced down at the rosemary again. Jazz pushed her way into his thoughts. He was so confused. He needed help.

Daisy.

Jazz.

Oh, God.

* * *

A knock on the door.

Gray turned to see Jazz at the back door, face peering through the glass pane in it. He glanced at the clock on the coffee maker where he'd just pressed the brew button. 9:00 a.m. Right on time. Daisy had been an on-the-dot type of person too.

He went to the door and opened it.

Jazz stood there, looking fresh and awake in a thick black sweater, eyes sparkling with excitement, the perfect combination with her black hair and alabaster skin. She had a small bag in her hand.

Wow, she looks great.

"Hi." She reached out and gave him a quick hug. "I smell coffee. Mmm. Delicious. I brought cranberry and banana nut muffins. I hope you're not allergic."

"No, banana nut is my favorite," he said.

"Perfect. Cranberry is mine. Now there won't be a fight." She laughed lightly and went over to the counter with the coffee maker. "Mugs? Plates?"

"Right above you," he said, still standing at the door, staring at her, marveling at her cheeriness and ease.

"You might want to close the door. It's not cold, but it is a bit chilly."

"Right." Gray came out of his daze. He'd missed her. Wait. How could he? He'd just met her. But he *had* missed her. There was something about her. Her energy. Her honesty.

And she was beautiful.

"After coffee and muffins, I'm going to set to work revitalizing your garden," Jazz said, breaking off the top of a muffin. "I brought some gardening tools, some minerals, sprays, fertilizer—"

"Uh, I have most of that," he interrupted her litany.

"Oh, I figured, but I have some… I guess you'd say, unorthodox 'vitamins' to help dying plants."

"Like…?"

"Coffee grounds, tea leaves…"

Gray laughed. "Well, it can't hurt, that's for sure. Good luck. If you need anything else there's a shed out back with more things, tools and stuff."

"Thank you. Do you know anything about Christmas plants?" Jazz took a bite out of her muffin top.

"Not much. That was Daisy's thing."

"I noticed, even though they were brown, that there were holly and ivy, and what I'm sure at one time was a magnificent Christmas cactus. There are a lot of others too. I'm not quite sure, given their sorry state, but I'll find out. I brought some of my plant books too."

Gray found himself laughing again. "Well if you can recognize them from all that dead crap, you must be pretty good."

"I am," she stated with absolute confidence.

"Then have at it. I thought we'd leave for the Washoe about 2:00. That'll give us a couple of hours for a drink and the tour."

"Perfect." And she took another huge bite of muffin.

* * *

"So you're not going to believe this, but…" Jazz paused for dramatic effect as she got into the passenger seat of Gray's truck. Gray closed it behind her and went to the other side.

"The Secret Garden's not as dead as you thought." She stared directly into Gray's eyes. "I see your skepticism, but it's true. And more than that… there are a couple of rare plants—at least for this area—that I wouldn't have thought could grow. Not to get too 'Three Wise Men' on you, but on some of those small trees there was dried up resin which could be frankincense or myrrh. Amazing! I also found poinsettias and amaryllis. Amaryllis... can you *believe it*? And I know I've got mistletoe, which I'm sure you don't know, but is a parasitic plant, order *Santalales*. I mention the order because the first part of it spells S-a-n-t-a: Santa! Coincidence or not? Anyway, Mistletoe attaches itself to other plants or shrubs. I've got some in the holly and the frankincense.

"The more I really inspected the plants, the more growth I found just waiting to flourish. Oh, Gray, it's so exciting!"

It had not gone unnoticed by Gray that Jazz kept using "I" in reference to "her" plants. Odd. But maybe not. Jazz was different. So excited and animated.

Like Daisy had been.

But Jazz was nothing like Daisy.

Not really.

"Yes, it's exciting." He nodded to her. Then the realization hit him: Yes, it *was* exciting!

And amazing.

"Well, I can hardly believe it," he said. "It's been five years. It was all dead—"

"Dormant," she corrected. "Just waiting for me, I guess."

She said it flippantly, but Gray wondered. Had she brought life to it? To him?

"So, changing the subject—but I may return to it—I was reading up on the Washoe Club last night, which was started after the Comstock Lode was discovered. It was decided that there would be sixty charter members in the club—all millionaires. Hence, the Millionaire's Club, as it is sometimes called," Jazz espoused, obviously proud of her research.

"I actually knew that." Gray smiled at her.

"Oh, sorry. But did you know that President Ulysses S. Grant, General Sherman, and Edwin Booth were members? *And* we're going to see a table in the Club where Grant and Mark Twain played cards together!"

Gray gave her a sheepish look. "I did," he said under his breath.

"Oh, you're no fun. Why did I spend hours on the computer? I should have just asked you." She had a spurious little girl pout on her face that Gray couldn't help but laugh at.

"Hours?" he asked through his chuckling.

"Well, maybe only an hour, but still…"

"I've only been on the tour once, but that part I remembered—about the cards. I'm a Twain fan. Or should I say Samuel Clemens?" He gave her a wink.

"Smarty. I knew that too. Oh, we're here!"

In front of them was a three-story, wooden and red-brick building. They got out of the truck and went up to the main door.

Gary held the door open for her, and she said, passing him, "Shall we have a drink in the haunted saloon before the tour? Maybe one of the three spirits will show up."

"No," gray said sternly.

Spinning around, Jazz said, "What do you mean, 'no'?"

"I mean… no, I didn't know there were three ghosts in the saloon." Now he smiled wryly. "Spirits with the spirits?"

She smacked him on the chest. "That was terrible. So, you don't know everything. That means you're buying." She turned away and sashayed over to the saloon area.

So much like her, he thought.

"Would you like a Bloody Brain or a Time Warp?" Gray asked her, reading from the specialty drink menu hanging above the bar. "I'm sure you'll *feel* the spirits then." He laughed at his pun.

Jazz groaned. "If your jokes don't get any better, then you won't have a *ghost* of a chance with me." She smiled pertly. "A Time Warp, please."

"Fine. I'll have the same. Then after the tour we can—"

"*Do the Time Warp agai-ain,*" she sang out loudly, causing the couple of other guests to stare their way.

"That *is* what I was going to say," Gray said. "But you *sang it* so much better." He turned to the bartender. "Two Time Warps, please."

The old, burly bartender gave Jazz a wink. "Nice singing, young lady. And it would be my pleasure if you'd come back and do the Time Warp *agai-ain.*" He made a half-hearted attempt at singing. "And when you're ready, the tour starts in the next room. It's… *just a jump to the left.*" He laughed heartily, and indeed did a jump to the left—all three hundred pounds of him.

Gray and Jazz laughed heartily along with him.

132

For the rest of the tour, Jazz held Gray's arm, and she touched him often. They saw the crypt and the mummified cat, but at the staircase that went nowhere is when it happened.

Jazz gasped. "Look!" She pointed to the top of the staircase.

Gray saw a quick movement. *A woman?* Then nothing. "Jazz, what is it?"

"Didn't you see her?" She stared at him. "I know you did. I can see it in your face. Blond hair, white dress, no shoes... about twelve or thirteen years old..."

"I don't know..." he said. *Blond, pretty... but older... she would look like... Daisy.*

"I *knew* you'd seen something. This is so fantastic! I felt during the whole tour that something was going to happen, and now right at the end of the tour... an honest-to-goodness *ghost*. I want to go up there. It's the tallest free-standing staircase, according to Ripley's." She glanced around. "No one's looking, Gray. Watch out for me. Here's my phone. Take a picture."

And before he could say anything, she'd bolted up the stairs. At the top, where it ended at the ceiling, she turned, smiled, and waved.

Gray raised the phone and took the picture.

"Aah!" he yelled.

There was Daisy again. Next to Jazz. No. *Part* of Jazz. He dropped the phone.

"*Gray,*" Jazz screamed and rushed back down the stairs. Several people came over from the other room to see what was happening.

"Everything all right?" someone said.

"Yeah, fine," Gray said, bending to pick up Jazz's phone.

Jazz reached out and put her hand on his arm. "Gray, are you sure you're OK? Did you see her again?" she said so no one could hear.

Gray didn't answer. People were still watching. "No, I'm fine." He raised his voice a little for the others' benefit. "I was just trying to scare her a little."

People smiled and nodded.

"Some scare," Jazz muttered.

Gray shot her a contrite look.

After the folks had cleared away, Jazz said, "You *did* see her again, didn't you?"

Gray slowly nodded.

Jazz grabbed her phone from her purse. "Maybe..." she hit the camera setting and stared at her phone. "*Ohmigod*," she whispered.

Gray felt a chill run up his spine. "What is it?"

She held out the phone to him.

Gray stared, open-mouthed. "No..."

There was the image of Jazz at the top of the stairs—a blond woman standing slightly behind her.

"That's not the little girl I saw," Jazz whispered. "Who could it be?"

"Daisy."

* * *

They were silent for a while on the ride back to Gray's.

Jazz finally broke their individual reveries. "Gray? What do you think it means?"

"I don't know," he said. Then, slamming the steering wheel, yelled, "I DON'T KNOW!"

Jazz gave a gasp at his outburst.

He quickly recanted. "I'm sorry, Jazz. I'm sorry. It's so hard to accept. It's so *weird*. Daisy's *gone*. She—"

"Maybe not." She put a hand on Gray's thigh, not intimately but in a comforting manner.

Gray glanced at her. "I need a drink. A stiff one. Maybe two."

She patted his leg. "I think that's a wonderful idea."

They sat on the couch in front of the fireplace. A few inches separated them as they imbibed their second bourbons. The air was electric with sexual tension.

"This was a good idea to heat them," Jazz said, taking a sip. "It does get cold at night. Between the fire and the bourbon, I'm good to go."

Gray had been staring at the fire, quietly sipping his own hot toddy. Mere inches away, he could feel her body heat, smell her perfume. He looked at her. Their eyes met, and the urge was too powerful to control. He closed the small gap between them and lowered his mouth to hers.

It was magic the moment their lips met. Gray tasted bourbon and... Jazz. Her taste was more intoxicating than the finest bourbon. It was Jazz infused. Her lips were soft, hot. Her tongue eased into his mouth. He wanted to cry out. She nibbled the inside of his lip. He felt himself stirring. It had been so long since he'd had this reaction. And it was instant. She set him on fire.

When their lips at last parted, he said, "There's a fireplace in the bedroom."

Her eyes burned as hot as the fire in front of them, and Gray was burning for her as well.

Jazz stood and took his hand. "Lead the way."

Gray knew as soon as he stood that his lust for her would be on prominent display. He stood.

Her eyes lowered, and she smiled seductively, hungrily.

Gray felt emboldened, powerful. He glanced down at himself. "It's been awhile."

"Too long, I think." She reached out and took hold of him, squeezing him in a mind-numbing way. The adept movement of her hand and fingers elicited a groan from him. She leaned into him, her ministrations becoming more adroit. "Kiss me," she said.

Gray leaned down. She bit on his upper lip and tugged his mouth to hers. He moaned louder now and felt the sensations growing stronger in his groin. Her tongue caressed and sucked his. He wanted to devour her. He felt pressure building as her hand moved more quickly, stroking, squeezing. He needed her to stop; he needed her to go on.

"Jazz, I..."

"Shh, you need this first." She stroked and squeezed harder. Her mouth and tongue working their magic. He was lost.

"Ahh, Jazz!" His body jolted as he released himself. She kept her hand moving while his orgasm played out, seemingly endless, his mouth and tongue ravenously, rapaciously assaulting hers.

His orgasm finished and his head in the crook of her neck, his ragged, rapid breathing gradually slowed. He felt like a teenager again, but even then he'd had more control. He'd never... come in his pants. How had she known that *was* what he needed? Now what?

"The bedroom?" she said, finally releasing her grip. "You start the fire, clean up... and we'll start our own fire again."

The look in her eyes hit him so hard he felt himself start to grow again. "This way." He grabbed her hand—perhaps a bit too firmly—but hey, he was a horny teenager again.

Jazz laughed. "Easy, Rambo, we've got all night. Save your big muscles for other things."

Rambo.

Daisy called him Rambo. And now he was hard again. Jazz.

And they did take all night. They explored and pleasured each other in every way. Whenever Gray felt hesitant to try something, Jazz would encourage him and go with it. She had found his most sensitive and favorite areas, and during their third—or maybe fourth—round, she had taken command and ridden him, and at the moment they climaxed together, she had taken his nipples in her fingers and rolled them around in such a way that he thrust up and exploded into her so violently that he thought she would be bucked right off him. But she wasn't. She had climaxed with him, screaming his name as she did. No one knew that he was so sensitive there and that it drove him crazy.

Almost no one.

The last time they made love he had wanted it to be all about her. He massaged, licked, sucked, stroked, teased. He got lost in his lovemaking, returning to all the techniques he'd employed over the years. She had responded to every one of them. But when he had begun to bite on her—oh-so-perfect—ass while his hand manipulated her in the front, she had cried out, "Now, Gray, bite me hard." He had bitten hard—not too hard—on one perfect round globe and she exploded around his fingers. "Yes, Gray, oh, my God!"

That's when it hit him.

Just like Daisy.

Everything. All he had done. She was just like Daisy. She enjoyed the *exact* same things. She said the same things. She'd know exactly what *he* liked: the rubbing, the stroking, his nipple fetish. It wasn't possible she could be *that* intuitive. Not *all* of it. How could she know?

Gray withdrew his hand. It was slick with her. Jazz gave a final gasp of pleasure as he eased out.

Dammit. Even though his head was as befuddled as could be, he was rock hard.

Jazz turned over to him. "Here, my turn. Let me take care of you now."

Gray wanted to protest, to say a hundred things, but as soon as her mouth touched him, every protestation was gone. Nothing but blissful pleasure.

* * *

136

Gray walked into the kitchen, the smell of bacon and pancakes redolent in the air. He knew it was pancakes and not waffles or French toast—because Daisy always made bacon and pancakes after a night of lovemaking. "Protein and carbohydrates," she'd said. And also...

"Mimosa?" Jazz said, coming over to him. She eased up onto her toes, kissed him and handed him a glass.

His lips responded automatically, and he took the glass. He stood frozen as she stepped back. "What's wrong?" she asked.

"Nothing," he responded. *Everything.* He drank. A big gulp.

"Uh huh, "she said. "The morning after. I get it. Well, you'll get over it. I also have a surprise. After breakfast. Which, by the way, is ready. Have a seat."

Gray obliged and sat at the fully set breakfast nook table. A pine frond sat in a vase at the center.

Daisy did that.

Don't freak out. Don't freak out.

"Here you go." Jazz sat a plate of three, six-inch-size pancakes in front of him and three corresponding bacon strips. Just like—

Jazz broke his thought. "And here's hot syrup." She set a small carafe next to him.

She got a similarly loaded plate for herself and sat. "I'm famished," she said. "You should be too, Rambo."

He couldn't take it anymore. "Jazz, please... I don't know what's happening, what's going on, but I need some time. Something... inexplicable is happening here... but it's impossible. I can't do this."

He saw a look of utter desolation cross her face. He was totally fucking this up. "Last night was great. Incredible. The best sex I've ever had. But you... you're not..."

"Daisy," she finished.

Gray was silent.

Jazz quietly got up and put down her napkin. She walked to the door, picked up her coat, put it on, and turned to him. "But I am."

And walked out.

* * *

Gray sat at the table for the next hour, stunned, not eating or drinking, just thinking.

Could it be? Had Daisy come back to him... as Jazz? Was Jazz possessed by Daisy? All answers were preposterous.

And yet...

Their lovemaking, the breakfast, the Washoe Club, the ghosts. The Garden.

Gray got up and went outside. It was cold. He went back inside and grabbed a jacket. It didn't help. His cold was coming from within.

He walked to the garden and stood outside the gate.

He couldn't go in. He couldn't bear to look. He thought he was falling in love with Jazz. But was he? Was it Daisy? No. They were so different.

He had to see for himself.

He opened the gate.

No.

Impossible.

The Secret Garden was in full bloom! Every plant flourished as they had on the best of days. Every plant. Everywhere.

The various fragrances assaulted his nostrils, almost making him choke with their pungency.

It was glorious.

"Gray?"

He looked to his left.

Jazz. Looking beautiful. But afraid.

"Jazz, how is this possible?"

"I'm not Jazz... Well, I am, but I'm Daisy too. She's here, kind of... inside me, I guess. It's hard to explain. I think it might be like a split personality type of thing, except that I know she's there. Like a guide. A coach. It's me, Jazz, but she gives me these subconscious tips. She doesn't overtly tell me anything. It's like a whisper. I don't feel her now. But I feel her here in the garden."

"I do too," Gray said, finally getting a coherent thought. "It's Christmas. She loved—loves?—Christmas. And her garden. The Secret Garden."

"This is awkward, but I think she approves, Gray," Jazz said, laying a hand on his arm. "I think she likes me..." She hesitated before saying, "...for you."

Gray studied her. He saw the fear in her face. He smiled to reassure her. "That would be just like her, watching out for me, wanting me to move on, to be happy. Maybe she guided you here.

Maybe she was waiting for you."

"But the garden…" she started.

"She wanted someone she could trust to take it over. Someone who could love and cherish it as she did. You loved it straight off, all brown and dead and everything. But you saw it alive and thriving. You had genuine excitement for it. And look… now it's what you saw it could be."

"Yes, it's beautiful."

Gray looked into her eyes. "Beautiful. You're beautiful. In every way. I see why Daisy chose you."

He saw the tears well up in her eyes. "But… you're still not sure. I understand." He could see she couldn't hide her feelings. "You're not sure how I feel, if it's all right. If only…" He jerked up. "Wait!" He darted away from her to the far side of the garden.

There it was.

"Oh, my God…," Jazz said as she reached him. "It's beautiful."

His rose. The Gray Rose. *His* rose.

She'd done it. An enormous, fully, opened blossom—as gray as it could be.

Her legacy.

Her blessing. She'd given it to him. To them.

A soft warm breeze wafted over them both.

"It's Daisy," Gray said. "She's saying goodbye. She can move on now." He felt the tears pour down his cheeks.

Jazz took his hand. "I can feel it too. I understand. So beautiful. Wonderful."

Gray turned her to him and smiled, seeing the look of understanding and jubilation on her face. He hoped he conveyed all the love he felt for her.

"We can move on now," he said.

"Yes, *we* can," Jazz said, taking both of his hands in hers and bringing them to her stomach.

He was puzzled.

He stared at her smiling, tear-stained face.

"Daisy said we should call them 'Holly' and 'Ivy'."

9

AQUA VITAE

Katherine Neville

In Xanadu did Kubla Khan
A stately pleasure-dome decree:
Where Alph, the sacred river, ran
Through caverns measureless to man
Down to a sunless sea... .

And mid these dancing rocks at once and ever
It flung up momently the sacred river.
Five miles meandering with a mazy motion
Through wood and dale, the sacred river ran,
Then reached the caverns measureless to man,
And sank in tumult to a lifeless ocean... .

That sunny dome! those caves of ice!
And all who heard should see them there,
And all should cry, Beware! Beware!

-Samuel Taylor Coleridge

Tuscany
1600s

In the year 1652, Ferdinando II was the Grand Duke of Tuscany. These were the waning years of the long and powerful rule of the Medici family of Florence. And Ferdinando, who was already a weak link in the chain, would not live to see his line decay into a dissolute and profligate stream of barbarians and wastrels.

Henpecked by his fat, ugly wife, Victoria della Rovere–fated to be outlived by progeny who would flood the Pitti Palace with drunkenness, lechery, gluttony, and homosexuality–Ferdinando himself had one redeeming grace. He was in love with science and spent every waking moment either in reading or discussing the subject. He had patronized the sciences as his forebears had squandered money upon the arts, bringing together at his court the great Galileo Galilei and many of his pupils in mathematics, astronomy and other sciences.

In May of 1652, the last of these, Vincenzo Viviani, was living at the Pitti Palace. Viviani was at this time thirty years of age and had succeeded Galileo as Engineer and Superintendent of the rivers of Tuscany. It was in this capacity that he was the first to be notified of the strange event–a miracle some called it–that had occurred on the banks of the Ombrone River, between Rome and Siena, on the first of May 1652.

* * *

"A great streak of light was seen in the sky," Viviani told Duke Ferdinando, as the two men rode out on horseback from Siena, surrounded by cavalry escort. "It is said to have been reddish in color and was witnessed by many of the country folk living in the outskirts of Siena. I have spent the morning interrogating them, and their stories are all consistent."

"I have heard of great stones that drop from the heavens," commented Duke Ferdinando, stroking his thick mustache and regarding the scientist with his great dark eyes. "Of course, to speak of such things is heresy…"

"The pope's mathematicians," smiled Viviani wryly, "have proven that stones cannot fall from the sky, because there are no stones in the sky. But when these nonexistent stones fall to earth, they often leave large craters in the ground, and the craters are lined with metals that, when tested, have no correlates that have ever been discovered on earth. Even the Greeks are said to have witnessed such phenomena. However, this case of the Ombrone River appears by all accounts to be completely different."

"In what manner?" asked Ferdinando, highly curious.

"When a stone falls from the sky, there is normally a flash of white light, followed sometime later by a deafening explosion. Witnesses can see and hear these manifestations, sometimes to a distance of twenty to thirty kilometers. Where the stone falls, as I've stated, there will be a pit lined in shiny metals. Often the grass and trees are scorched for hectares around the site. This is not true of the case on the Ombrone.

"The witnesses, my lord, all report that there was no sound of any type. There was merely a slow streak of red light, pale but luminous like a rainbow, passing in a long arc from the heavens to the earth. It lasted for many hours, from the late night into the early morning. As it happens, many people were abroad at that hour, due to the May Day festivities, and all were witnesses. The next morning, they went to where they believed the streak had come down. And there they found not a hole, but a long strip of something lying beside the river. Uniform in length and width, it was about fifty meters by one hundred, and composed of a resinous or gelatinous paste that seemed luminous. It smelled to some faintly of sulfur. To others, the odor seemed sweetish. But we will see it soon. It is just down there."

He motioned to a place below them on the riverbank, where neatly groomed rows of ancient olive trees with twisted trunks and silver leaves ran over the rolling hills to the river. Even from this distance, they could see the strip of white, exposed like a gash against the red earth; it glowed along the wide allée lying between the olive groves. Motioning the cavalry escort to halt, the scientist Viviani and Duke Ferdinando headed their horses down the soft embankment.

At the bottom, near the edge of the river, the two men dismounted their horses and moved carefully to the edge of the strip of white; from this close perspective, the milky mass glowed even more brightly, with an incandescent light. It lay in a broad swath, completely covering the flat ground to a depth of five or six centimeters. It was gelatinous, like the white of an uncooked egg, and gave off a sickeningly sweet odor that was hard to identify.

"Whatever can this be?" said Duke Ferdinando in wonder, prodding a patch gingerly with the toe of his boot.

"I cannot say, my lord," replied the other, kneeling upon the ground to examine the mass more closely. "But I shouldn't touch it until we've had the chance to study a small amount beneath a lens. It may prove in some manner dangerous."

"In all my years of studying science," said the duke, "I have never seen nor heard of anything like it upon the face of our whole broad earth."

"Nor I," said Viviani, regarding the duke with a strange expression. They held each other's gaze for a long moment before bending to the task.

Viviani collected sixty samples in glass jars, to carry to his laboratory in Florence. These were carefully handled and labeled at the site, in preparation for the return journey.

But the next morning, when they were ready to depart, the scientist checked the bottles and discovered that the contents of all had evaporated, though each had been hermetically sealed. Returning to the river site with an escort, he saw that the luminous swath of the day before had also vanished–melted, perhaps, into the earth. There was no trace at all of its existence.

This was the first recorded sighting.

* * *

Sightings
1700s to 1900

It was sixty-six years before another sighting was reported, in a remote part of India in the year 1718. And another seventy-eight years passed before, in 1796, a small town along the Tagus River on the Iberian Peninsula reported another. After that, the sightings came more frequently–or perhaps it was only that communications had improved, and strange matters of this sort were being more carefully reported and preserved. But the descriptions were always the same, though as time progressed, some details were added.

It was noticed, for example, that for several days prior to an event, a smallish but very dark cloud would appear in the sky above the location in question, remaining stationary with no wind, while the rest of the sky was completely clear. Then late one night, near midnight, a red streak would appear in the sky and slowly extend itself until it seemed to touch the earth. The following morning, the local inhabitants would discover the mass.

It was always described as white or greyish-white, translucent, jelly-like, and slightly luminous. It was rarely more than three hundred feet in length, and often smaller. It was only a few inches deep, sometimes lying in lumps or clots, sometimes in pea-shaped balls. It came down in the heat of summer or in the dead of winter, even falling upon firmly-packed snow. It fell in France, Germany, Sweden, and even on the eastern seaboard of the United States, in New York and New Jersey. Two things were always precisely the same: the places where it fell were always near a river that fed the ocean. And the mass was always gone by the morning following the original sighting.

That was the case, at least, until the morning of July 8, 1841.

That was the morning when the town of Derby, England, near the Trent River was shut down because of the frogs.

* * *

"Never seen nothing like it," reported Mr MacLeish, a local pub-keeper who had resided in Derbyshire for over forty years. "It was lump ice, some in the shape of cubes like billiard chalk, some pieces so big they was six or seven inches across, and that ain't no exaggeration. If you don't believe me, ask Homer Smith about it. He blames it for killing two of his sheep. Not to say as I fancies sheep myself. Filthy animals, if you ask me. But it's the size of it what I was commenting upon. And not a cloud in the sky, five minutes before it hit us…

"Then of course," he added, scratching his shaggy head, "there was them frogs."

A week later, on July 15, the London Times reported: "A sudden shower of half-melted ice struck a town in Derbyshire last week, ruining many crops and killing a few animals. The residents of the county report that embedded in some pieces of ice were small green frogs, resembling tree frogs, many of which survived."

"They told us," said Horace Smith of Derby, "that the same thing happened over in France nearly fifty years ago. A big black cloud suddenly appeared from nowhere, high up in the sky, and it started raining little green frogs. All over the ground, they was, though none of them lived that time. But what do you expect, in France? That's a country of frogs, you know. That's where most of them likely came from. But ours have lived, some of them, though they're a mite sickly. But what do you expect, when they were all frozen in lumps of ice? If they'd of been healthier, we might of ate 'em ourselves!"

* * *

In July 1873, the Scientific American reported a shower of frogs falling upon Kansas City, Missouri, on the Missouri River. In 1882, in the middle of June, the ironworks at Dubuque, Iowa on the Mississippi River was showered in ice containing small baby frogs, some of which were still breathing. In July of 1883, the London Times again reported showers of frogs: in the Apennines, France, and Tahiti. In November of the same year, Scientific American noted showers of frogs in Ohio and Puerto Rico. The same magazine reported that in August of the prior year an eighty-pound block of ice had landed in Salina, Kansas, which lies between two forks of the Kansas River. These tributaries do not directly feed the ocean, but Salina itself is built on the bed of a large salt lake which is believed once to have been an inland sea. The bodies of small frogs were embedded in the block of ice.

But something had gone wrong. Before the great rains of frogs up and down the rivers of the world that occurred in the 1880s, something happened that had nearly gone unnoticed, though it received small mentions in both the Scientific American and the New York Times in the year 1876.

On March 3, 1876, something fell to earth in Bath County, Kentucky, situated near Licking Creek. But Licking is not a river and it does not feed the sea. It is a small creek, a dry bed in summer, that meanders through northern Kentucky, forty miles from the Ohio, the nearest river. And what fell into Bath that day was neither jelly-like matter nor blocks of ice—nor were there any little green frogs in evidence. It was described as something resembling beef. Big, flesh-colored flakes of beef.

Doctors examined it. Some said it was lung tissue, others said it was cartilage or muscle fiber. Scientific American sent a scientist who examined it and declared that it was nostoc, a type of algae that lives in atmospheric nitrogen. He neglected to mention that nostoc had never fallen from the skies in large flakes, or that it is blue-green in color.

These flakes did not disappear. In a few days, the flakes dried out until they were dark brown and resembled beef jerky. But no one tried to eat them. The scientists dubbed it "The Kentucky Phenomenon." It was never mentioned again.

* * *

Shortly after the Kentucky Phenomenon took place, the wheels started to appear. In May of the year 1880, a steamer was cruising through the Persian Gulf. It was about 11:30 pm when the bosun on duty noticed a glow coming from beneath the water. He summoned the captain and the two men studied the phenomenon closely from the foredeck.

Two large wheels with slowly moving spokes were revolving on either side of the ship. They gave out a luminous glow from beneath the water. They followed alongside the ship until it reached the open sea, then slowly disappeared into the depths.

One month later, on June fifth, the same wheel images were sighted off the Malabar coast of India in the Arabian sea, not far from the first sighting. It was 10:00 at night, and the wheels remained beside the steamer for two hours. At midnight, they drifted away across the sea. A few moments later, three large balls of fire rose from the water and headed off into the sky.

After these events, these "landings" became more sophisticated, more frequent, and more focused:

After the year 1883, ice was no longer used.

After the year 1885, the frogs were white.

* * *

In August of 1889, Savoy France—lying on a tributary of the Rhone river—reported a shower of small white frogs falling from a cloudless sky. July 30 of 1892, white frogs fell upon Birmingham England, on the Trent. In August of 1894, they fell upon Wigan in

146

Manchester, on a tributary of the Mersey, which dumps into the Irish Sea. In the same month, they saw a new phenomenon at Bath on the Thames, not far from the Bristol Channel. It was not the first time something like this had happened at Bath; it was the second. The first had been twenty-three years earlier.

* * *

"I was only a boy at the time," said Charles Perkins, a porter on the railroad and a resident of Bath from childhood. "It was twenty-three years ago in April. I've kept the newspaper clippings from the London Times: April 24, 1871. But it happened two days earlier. It was a perfectly clear day, not a cloud in the sky. Suddenly, this jelly-like glop started falling from the sky. It fell all over the roof of the railway station here. Came down for nearly half an hour, just as has happened yesterday.

"We went outside with ladders, all the townsfolk, and started scraping it off the roof. At first, we thought maybe it was a freak ice storm, but there wasn't any ice. It was this goo that sort of stuck to everything. But the funny thing was, it started to hatch. Just like yesterday. And these wormlike things, you know, these little worms or sort of whitish tadpoles, they started hatching out. We didn't know what they were, so we just shoveled them onto the ground and buried them."

They were like chrysalises, from small eggs contained in thick jelly. But not microscopic this time. They were large enough to see. They hatched out at Bath, at Eton Bucks, at many locations in England and France. But people scraped them off and buried them without investigating what they might be.

* * *

1900 to the Present

During the 1920s the frogs fell again. This time they came in rainstorms and the falls lasted longer. They fell in July of 1921 at Sterling, Connecticut not far from the Connecticut Thames that feeds Block Island Sound. In August they fell in London on the other Thames. In September of 1922, the London Daily News reported that they fell for two whole days upon Chalon-sur-Seine in France. In

March of 1925 there was a report from the Transvaal, South Africa, of a shower of frogs along the Orange River that empties into the Atlantic Ocean; in April 1927, another report of a similar phenomenon along the Russian River in northern California, leading to the Pacific Ocean.

Then nothing—for more than two years.

In October of 1929, a small mention appeared on a back page of the Reno Nevada Gazette: three sightings had been reported individually by natives in the remote mountain regions around Lake Tahoe, who'd each observed a mysterious, gelatinous substance that coated the riverbanks and oozed into the waters of the American River's north, middle, and southern forks. These three separate forks of the river hurtle down from the mountains near the California/Nevada border, ultimately converging to join the Sacramento River in its long course to the San Francisco Bay and the Pacific Ocean.

This report was not picked up by any journals, scientific or otherwise, for the simple reason that only a few weeks later the legendary stock market crash would begin—"Black Tuesday"— leading to the global depression that would preoccupy the rest of the world for the next thirteen years.

But one man, high atop a hill in San Francisco, was not so preoccupied. For decades he'd been following—through private clipping services in many lands—the reports of these strange sightings around the world. (Through his travels, he himself was fluent in seven languages.) These reports were usually relegated to the back pages of an obscure journal like this one. Reading the tiny article on the back page of this local Nevada paper, he smiled privately.

Then he picked up his hat and silver-headed cane, went to the garage where he stepped into his sparkling new Duesenberg J Phaeton racing car—one of only two hundred minted in the world— and drove himself to his broker's office on California Street. There, he quietly placed an order to liquidate all fifty million dollars of his stocks, bonds, and commodities investments, and to buy Canadian gold bullion with the proceeds. Then he contacted his personal pilot to prepare a flight plan for Nevada, and wired his real estate broker with the following message:

"Buy all the land on the eastern shore of Lake Tahoe."

Success was merely a question of knowing where the action was, and when to act. As a boy, he'd turned his back on his family's stodgy Nob Hill life and their millions, to run off with the Barnum and Bailey Circus and travel the world. Now, as the world was about to collapse around him, he knew once again where the action would be.

According to all reports, they'd been attempting a landing for five hundred years, hadn't they? He wanted to be there–to be at the center of things, to be in control–when they finally succeeded.

* * *

Lake Tahoe, Eastern Shore, Winter: The Present

Mindy Berry, the young postdoctoral student accompanying the expedition, gazed from her perch on the stone terrace of Thunderbird Lodge as the sun set over the vast, shimmering expanse of the turquoise lake. Not a cloud disturbed the sky, not a ripple shattered the mirrored water. All the tourists, at this time of year, were up in Squaw Valley skiing or holed up in the casinos far from here. Here on the eastern shore, you could almost hear the silence.

Mindy was more than concerned about that silence: it had been seven long hours, with no word, since her companions had departed in their private boat to study the lake's pristine eastern shoreline. She'd been left here at the lodge, as their contact point with the outside world–though as yet there'd strangely been no contact in any direction. She tried one more time to raise the boat by her satellite phone. To no avail.

The disparate group of scientific specialists, including Mindy herself, had been beckoned here from around the globe– unobtrusively, at a moment's notice–to report upon an extremely curious phenomenon. One that was being kept under a tight lid, in more ways than one.

The formidable list of men who'd departed the lodge this morning on their long-absent boat–along with their millions of dollars in sophisticated equipment–included a noted oceanographer from Scripps Institution of Oceanography in California; as well as an ocean floor spectrometry expert from Woods Hole in Massachusetts; a renowned microbiologist from the Smithsonian Tropical Research Institute in Panama; a climatologist and a marine biologist from the National Oceanic and Atmospheric Research Administration; a geophysicist along with a topologist from the US Geological Survey. And two famous hydro-geologists who'd supervised Mindy's own doctoral dissertation—undoubtedly the very reason that she, a mere minion among these scientific gods, had been invited along for the ride.

But Thunderbird Lodge was an odd choice, Mindy thought, for this private conference of "scientific observers." Though it did have a private boathouse and a 600-foot-long stone tunnel, blasted into the rock, that served to mask arrivals and departures.

The very history of the place was steeped in mystery: the lodge had been built during the Great Depression by the San Francisco playboy millionaire, "Captain" George Whittell, who (before he'd turned into a famous recluse) had been a collector of many exotic things, such as: glamorous "showgirl" wives and lovers; expensive cars, planes and yachts; eccentric friends, from Hemingway to Howard Hughes; and outré pets, from Mingo the elephant, to Bill the lion, to a boa constrictor named Pete.

Mindy couldn't repress the nagging thought that had plagued her ever since she'd arrived here at the lodge: Why would one of America's richest men, nearly a hundred years ago, liquidate his significant assets—cash in his chips, only moments before he might have lost them all in the stock market crash—and then invest everything he'd seemingly rescued, into this remote and nearly worthless piece of lakefront property? Why would he spend the next ten years building a "summer home" on a pile of boulders, just to create a private, hidden retreat, and escape from his glamorous world of glitterati—from the only world George Whittell had ever known?

Why indeed.

But from a scientific viewpoint, the most important thing that George Whittell had collected was this clandestine acquisition: piece after piece, over several years, of what would eventually amount to 95% of the eastern shoreline of America's largest and deepest alpine body of water: Lake Tahoe.

Indeed, Tahoe, bordered by California and Nevada, contained one of the greatest volumes of water of any lake in America, and was ranked among the deepest lakes in the world.

It was the depth that intrigued her.

That was undoubtedly the reason that Mindy Berry herself had been called here, to this precise spot, to meet with the unholy secret alliance of scientific explorers.

Growing up, as Mindy had, in a family of West Virginia miners, she'd been exposed from early childhood to the mysteries that lay a mile or two beneath the surface of the earth. Especially the mysteries of deep and hidden waters.

When Mindy was eight years old, her miner uncle Ned had been washed through five miles of a collapsed mineshaft, where an underground river had broken through and had demolished the supporting infrastructure of the mine.

He'd lived to tell the tale:

"Water is more powerful than man," Ned said, "more powerful than rock. A simple river carved out the Grand Canyon. Glaciers grind mountains of granite into bits. Water is a silent force that can eat its way through anything."

Mindy never forgot about the power of water. She'd studied it all her life. Her science dissertation defense, only last year, had raised plenty of eyebrows in the scientific world. Especially coming, as it did, in the midst of the huge global-political debate on whether so-called "climate change" was: 1) a figment of our collective, harebrained, indoctrinated imaginations, versus: 2) a totalitarian conspiracy of zillionaires plotting to control the world's supply of natural resources, such as potable water.

Her dissertation defense...?

Both scenarios might just be true!

She'd documented, analyzed, often even visited and examined, deep repositories of water around the globe: aquifers spanning vast spaces beneath the earth; underground rivers that were buried in the wild by nature, or beneath cities, by man; pockets of water trapped for millennia in ancient mines and caves; frozen lakes in Antarctica, held hostage by blocks of ice; reservoirs saltier than seawater, though they were far inland from any sea...

—And all these imprisoned bodies of water were like a life force, held under pressure, just waiting to explode and be freed from their earthly tombs;

—And all these bodies of water were also alive in a different way: teeming with living organisms that that had learned to survive under the direst of conditions!

That was precisely why Mindy Berry–the only young scientist who'd spent her entire life like Orpheus visiting the Underworld–was so concerned about the ongoing (now nearly 8-hour) absence of her world-class colleagues, the top experts in deep water and its multiple, ancient life forms.

They had departed here this morning to investigate the one place where reports suggested that these two strange worlds might just have collided: here on the eastern shore. Scanning the horizon as darkness fell, Mindy tried her satellite phone again.

Not one ripple disturbed the surface of the lake.

Not a sound broke the silence of the air.

* * *

Operation River Styx: On the Sinkhole and Underground Waterway
beneath Lake Tahoe, Nevada

White Paper submitted to the President of the United States,
By Directive of the National Oceanic and Atmospheric Research Administration

Presented by Melinda Berry, PhD, ScD
Mr. President,
As you have been informed, our operational vessel that was investigating the strange occurrence on Tahoe's eastern shore has vanished, with all men and equipment, into what is now thought to be an enormous sinkhole created by a heretofore unknown underground river beneath the lake floor. There has been no communication with that vessel or its occupants since it departed from berth one week ago.

Ten days ago, a large plume of water had been reported spewing just off the eastern shore of Lake Tahoe. It was filmed briefly from the land, by a lone nature photographer: the plume seemed to exceed more than sixty feet in height, and behave much like a geyser, though monitors around the lake had recorded no seismic activity or other disturbance on the lake's floor. When the plume dissipated, the same photographer observed a mass out in the water that looked like a very large person or animal with fins or flippers, swimming toward shore. He tried to film it, but his camera went dead. All of the power lines along that stretch of the lake went dead, and they remained dead thereafter, for more than eight hours.

This is the sixth report of a plume of water from the lake, followed by a sighting of an unknown person or being, in froglike gear, swimming in the vicinity. This film of the water plume was saved into the Cloud, however, and it remains the first hard evidence we have of unusual aquatic activity reported in these parts–evidence that prompted our investigative mission dubbed "Operation River Styx." (The Styx being the mythical underground river that Greeks believed separated Earth from Hades, and which was the passageway of dead souls into the underworld.)

As for actual underground waters, the topic of this report: The National Oceanic and Atmospheric Administration (NOAA) has long estimated that more than 97% of earth's water lies in the oceans and seas that circle our globe, while less than 3% of water–what we drink and pollute and use for irrigation—comes from rivers, streams, springs, glaciers, lakes, and groundwater in the form of wetlands and underground aquifers.

Based upon our recent findings in the Lake Tahoe basin, the present report challenges those statistical conclusions.

Deep "paleowater"–or fossil water–exists far under the earth's surface, even beneath high mountain lakes like Tahoe or underneath the ocean's floor. Some of this water has been found miles deep, trapped in rock, and is millions of years old. Microbes and multi-cell organisms can live where there is water: in rocks, in frozen lakes, even in solid ice. Likewise, under pressure and heat, they can survive in pockets where conditions, and chemicals, are similar to hydrothermal vents able to support life on the deepest ocean floor.

These deep bodies of water are often connected to one another, miles below the earth's surface, and they provide a passage-a waterway, running beneath lakes, forests, even cities-that has been used for millennia by microorganisms and even more highly evolved life forms.

What if one of those highly-evolved life forms chose to become amphibian...?

* * *

Mindy, still at work at her desk in the science lab, looked at her computer for a long moment, studying what she'd written so far. Then she highlighted everything she'd put down in her report so far—except for her initial address to the President. She took a very deep breath. Then she gingerly touched the "delete" button. The text vanished—just as swiftly and thoroughly as that ship full of important scientists had, one week ago. Was it just one week? It seemed an aeon now.

Life that existed in the waters beneath the earth, and under the sea, was so astonishingly beautiful. Aqua Vitae, they called it: Living Water. And the waters in the depths of the earth truly were alive!

In the deep waters off Japan, she'd seen creatures shimmering in darkness, creating their own phosphorescent colors to light their world. In Panama, she'd seen newly-evolving species where the Atlantic, Pacific and Caribbean came together. Creatures formed in the womb of ancient water beneath the earth were like a miracle. What had enabled them to survive, to grow as they had?

They'd been mutating into amphibians: that she understood. They had to—for how could they exist, once we'd tapped all the underground storage of water, accumulated in the earth, that had been their life blood over millions of years?

Mindy sighed.

Then she began her letter to the president once again:

Dear Mr. President-

Given the existence of the following conditions that I've reported upon: the depth of Lake Tahoe, at more than 1600 feet; the sudden disappearance of our ship, containing key scientists and priceless scientific equipment; and the sighting, only three days previous to that, of a water plume and of frogmen on the lake-it appears clear that there is only one explanation:

The Russians, or other governments bent upon ill intent, have found an underwater access and egress for small submarines or aquatic vehicles to penetrate, and lie hidden and unobserved, near the unpopulated eastern shore of Lake Tahoe.
Our scientific ship has fallen into the hands of an unscrupulous foreign agent. As a deep-water scientist, I'd be honored to assist our government in exploring the lake floor to help discover how these nefarious people gained access.

Mindy pressed the "send" button, which would place her report into the hopper at NOAA for its review. They wouldn't believe a word of it, of course, nor would the President–if he ever got to see her cockeyed explanation in the first place.

But it would buy her the time that she needed.

After all, she was the only person who knew what lived in those deep waters.

10

HAVEN

Charissa Weaks

"It is the thing we cannot see that will be our doom. The monster, hidden in our midst, that dormant, unnatural essence inside us all. Some days, the loneliness and longing are too much, and I crave death. But death is a lie now because we come back. Different. Hungry. Cunning. Cold. Therein lies my conundrum. If I die, I become the illusory being of despair and misery I despise. If I live, my days will fill with growing fear as I await my inevitable and violent end. But I cannot live forever, damn it. I cannot live forever."
-From the Journal of Samuel Tucker Morgan
Haven's Landing, Old Reno
Summer, 2418

Sam lifted his glass of whiskey so the deputies could heave the dead boy's corpse onto the bar.

"Damn it to Hell," was all he could manage to say. He despised corpses. That this one was a kid, no more than sixteen, was bad. That he wasn't one of their own, even worse. That he made number three in as many days?

A nightmare.

Sam had hoped his men would arrive with reports of an uneventful day. Instead, they'd brought him what he already knew this kid symbolized: a final warning.

Blue eyes stared at him, frozen wide and round in horror. The boy's mouth hung half-open, lips twisted, contorting his countenance

156

into a death scream. A person's last moments had to be terrifying to carve such a powerful final expression.

Sam swallowed hard, a chill frosting his bones. He remembered a face like that.

Settling a pleading gaze on his men, he said, "Tell me you didn't find him on the Limits."

Perkins wiped sweat from his upper lip, body quivering. "I w-wish I could, sir."

"Was he alive when you found him?"

"No," Jed replied. "I spotted him climbing the boundary before sundown. I grabbed Perkins and went to collect him, but we were too late. Looks like dehydration. Saw him from Miss Ella's watchtower."

The sound of Ella's name made Sam's body ache with longing. If he could protect anyone from learning about the last few days, it was Ella Kincaid. Her loft sat above the town Athenaeum, a three-storied structure whose bell tower served as a lookout.

Sam worked to keep his voice unaffected. "Does she know about this?"

"No, sir." Jed removed his hat and rubbed his balding head. "Kept quiet, as you asked."

The people of Haven's Landing weren't ready for this kind of disaster. Most had never witnessed what Sam had. They'd only heard stories, and the disconnect between hearing a tale and living it proved too great a divide. Perkins was evidence of that truth. They were all too young to remember the world ending, but Jed and Sam had seen what happened to the dying upon their final breath. In a time of no disease, when lifespans grew longer, it took an act of nature, starvation, or some fatal wound to end a life, unless something worse came first. Perkins had faced the dead boy's newborn wraith, the being's most nonhazardous state, and the experience still shook him to his core.

Sam sat his glass aside and stood. Gently, he gripped Perkins by the back of the neck. "It's all right. Don't let it eat at you."

Perkins' face paled, even under his sunburn. "It c-came out of him, sir. L-like a demon. It looked at me. It chased us and screamed off into the desert and—"

Sam handed him his whiskey. "Drink. It'll calm you."

All humans gave up the ghost. Once upon a time, the entity that left a body had been known as a soul, bound for Heaven or Hell. But things changed, a consequence of a time when angels and demons battled, and demons won. Now souls were wraiths, the living dead. The afterlife no longer existed, unless one considered becoming a havoc-wreaking specter an afterlife.

Sam turned back to the dead boy. The smell of sweat, sun-scorched flesh, and death made his stomach crawl into his throat. Still, he inspected the body, from ragged clothes to near-sole-less boots. No wounds existed, save for lesions from the sweltering sun and sand. The harsh terrain of the West killed easily enough, but something terrible had driven people from their coastal communes in desperation. Sam feared he knew what that something was.

"Did he say anything?" he asked.

The men went silent, but then Perkins spoke. "H-he said, *'they're coming. A horde. Hide.'*"

Sam gripped the counter and lowered his head to temper the panic clenching his torso like a vise.

Jed's voice trembled. "Think he meant Grievers, sir?"

Sam did think that, but he couldn't speak it into the universe yet. Newborn wraiths eventually joined packs, better known as hordes. He hadn't faced a group of those wailing bastards in years, but a throng would soon cross the mountain range that'd shielded Haven's Landing for decades. Bounded by desert on one side, the Pacific and the Sierra Nevada on the other, their town had been encapsulated from harm. But if Grievers followed the drifters' path, Haven's refuge would be in their sights, an oasis for dead beings searching for life.

A groan pulled on Sam's focus.

His friend, Ren, had stepped from the back room carrying a crate of glassware. "You gotta be kidding me, Sam. Again? This is a saloon, not a morgue."

"We could do this at the City Café," Sam replied. "If you prefer chaos."

Ren's was the best place for Sam to rendezvous with his men at day's end. No one would question him visiting his best friend after hours, and no one would venture that far so late at night. It didn't hurt that the tavern had a plot of sandy land on its south side, making it a perfect burial ground for drifters.

Ren sat the crate on the counter. "I just want this over. Shit's getting scary now. Jed just said 'Grievers', didn't he?"

Sam rubbed his face. "Unfortunately." He looked at his men. "Say nothing to anyone, not even your wives. We don't need this spreading tonight. I'll figure out a plan and deal with things come morning."

"But, sir," Perkins said. "What if—"

"'What if' nothing. Do as I say. Bury the body, then go home to your families. We're safe. If a horde were coming, we'd know it. They can be heard from miles away."

The men looked swallowed by fear, but obediently grabbed the body and headed out the back door. Sam slipped on his hat, a million worries ricocheting through his mind.

"What are you gonna do?" Ren asked. "Fuck. What are *we* gonna do?"

Sam planted his hands on his hips. "I don't know. People will run if we don't handle it right, and if they flee, there's nothing any of us can do for them."

He thought about the children, imagined them suffering in the desert because he hadn't eased their parents' hysteria. Grievers came for the weak, fearful, and broken-hearted. Sometimes they left people mad. Sometimes they sucked all emotion from their veins. And sometimes, they added to their numbers, leaving innocents behind.

Sam knew that all too well.

Heart heavy as a sinking stone, he turned to go. "Night, Ren. Hold your family close. We'll talk in the morning."

"You're a good man, Sam Morgan," Ren called. "But even you can't save everyone."

"Yeah," Sam replied. "That's what I'm afraid of."

* * *

Sam kicked up dust as he walked down an empty Main Street toward home. The town had fallen silent, except for the crickets chirping in the distance. The night winds were still, the air thick with the scent of earth and heat.

As usual, his gaze went to Ella's place. She'd been all he'd thought about for so long. Two years earlier, her husband left for Vegas on a supply expedition and never returned. After a year of giving Ella her space, Sam found his courage and ended up in her library daily, wishing he knew what to do with all his feelings for her.

With a sigh, he glanced at the full moon, then noticed lights

159

twinkling in windows above the Sundries and City Café. He thought about checking on the merchants, but a screen door banged from behind, and a velvet voice stopped him cold.

"Some people never sleep."

Ella.

Heavy as his burdens were, Sam couldn't help but grin. He turned to find her leaning against a post on her crooked porch, creamy skin kissed by the moon's glow. He closed the distance between them, etching the inviting image of her into his mind, from bare feet to the sweet curve of full breasts silhouetted under her cotton gown, to that cold black hair tumbling down her shoulders. His mouth watered.

"I was heading home, thank you very much," he replied.

"Mhmm." She folded her arms. "Anything interesting keeping you out so late, Sheriff?"

He reached the porch and stood below her, trying not to let the night's worries bleed onto his face. Propping his foot on a step, he peered into her sea-green eyes from under the brim and shadow of his hat. She had no idea how interesting things had been. He wanted to tell her everything, but—

Christ. If she ran...

He'd stop her. He'd beg her to let him protect her, even though she had no reason to place her trust in him. Haven had been so quiet for so long; he'd never saved anyone. Why would she put her life in his hands? Why would any of Haven's citizens?

He inhaled deep to wash away the thoughts. "I grabbed some whiskey over at Ren's. What about you? Why aren't you cozied up reading?"

She inched closer, until the billowing fabric of her gown brushed against him. "Sleep eludes me yet again," she said. "Who knows the reason tonight. Maybe the moon is too bright or the world too still." She shrugged a delicate shoulder. "It's just hard being in that empty loft alone. Sometimes a woman needs a pair of arms to hold her."

Sam ran a damp palm down the side of his jeans. He never knew what to say when Ella spoke that way. He couldn't tell if she still mourned her husband, or if her subtle mentions of loneliness meant she'd grown tired of being alone and wanted the town's Sheriff to rectify the situation. He wished he understood women because if that's what she wanted, he had perfectly good arms for the job.

He swallowed the lump in his throat. "Anything I can do to help?"

The balmy night air pulled a sheen of sweat across Ella's skin. She stared down at him, the angle giving him a tempting view of her throat. Her hair moved, its lavender and honey aroma teasing him. A man could lose himself for days inside a woman like Ella, and Sam desperately wanted to prove that theory.

She touched his face, fingertips running through the two-day growth covering his jaw. Sam's heart stopped. She'd never touched him before, unless accidentally bumping him in the library counted. He'd craved the feel of her skin on his, longed for her to invite him inside the Athenaeum where he'd lay her down between Classics and Modern and obliterate their loneliness.

He leaned into her touch. "Ella, what are you doing?"

She kissed the corner of his mouth. "Forgive me," she whispered, her breath sweet and clean on his face. "You've been so patient." Her thumb trailed across his lips. "Soon."

Soon.

His body blazed hot as the sun at all the possibilities that one word implied. But he didn't know if they had soon. He didn't even know if they had tonight.

He held her gaze, trying to let the sliver of hope piercing his heart take root. "Just say when. You know where to find me." He pulled her hand from his face, her slender fingers disappearing inside his rough grip. "Do me a favor?"

She searched his face to decipher the hint of worry he knew betrayed him. "Of course."

"Lock your doors tonight. Fasten your shutters."

She looked taken aback. No one secured anything in Haven. "Why? What's wrong?"

He shook his head, wishing he could tell her, but the consequences scared him. He had to keep her there, at least until the cloak of night left the world. It was safer to tell her come daylight. Daylight made surviving feel more possible.

"Nothing's wrong," he answered. "I just need to know you're safe."

If Grievers *did* come in the night, such protections served no purpose. The natural world held no boundaries for phantoms, but he had to hope they'd pass her by if they couldn't see her. Sometimes

161

the force of their presence blew open unlocked doors, shattered glass from windows, and the screams of those hiding lured the wraiths inside.

If that happened...

If they felt her...

He felt sick. Grievers loved a mourning heart, and he worried Ella had grief in spades.

"Promise me," he added.

Tenderly, she rubbed his furrowing brow. "I promise. But we're discussing this tomorrow, all right?"

He agreed and brought her hand to his mouth. Slowly, he kissed a trail from her fingertips to her little wrists where her pulse pounded against his lips. Then, though it caused an ache in every cell, he turned and headed toward home.

* * *

Sam never made it to his homestead. He tried, but halfway out he doubled back and climbed Ella's watchtower. If he couldn't be in her bed, he could be on her roof concocting a plan while watching the blue-black horizon for any sign of movement.

Sometime before dusk, when the bruised sky gives way to rose-tinted light, Sam drifted to sleep. When he opened his eyes, Ella sat at his side, leaning over him, her hair curtaining them as she stared into his eyes. He slid his hand into the black veil, and like all his dreams of her before, he pulled her to him.

Ella kissed him achingly slow. He returned her kiss with every ounce of desire that had built inside him over those last months. He'd imagined what she might taste like so many times. Honey. Sweet wine. Spun sugar.

He'd been wrong.

She tasted like bliss, sun and light and... love.

He kissed her like a dying man, as though he'd never get the chance again, but she nipped his lip, and he stopped, the gentle pain sobering him.

She drew away and smiled. "Morning, Sheriff."

Adrenaline shot through him. Startled, still in defense mode and half asleep, he scrambled to sit up.

Ella took his hand in hers and gripped his chin. "Hey, hey." Her focused eyes caught his darting gaze. "It's just me. I didn't mean to scare you."

He glanced around to get his bearings, felt the morning breeze rustle his hair, licked the dampness from Ella's mouth off his lips.

It was real. He'd finally kissed her properly, yet it seemed like a dream.

"I'm so sorry." He shook his head in disbelief. "I never would've done that if I'd been—"

Ella pressed a finger to his mouth, her cheeks pinking. "Stop. It's okay. If you couldn't tell, I loved it."

Sam scrubbed a hand through his hair, speechless. He reached for his hat, unsure what else to do with his hands. His face burned, too.

She loved it.

How cruel the universe could be. He'd made it to the precipice of her heart's door and now had to level her world and hope she'd still let him in afterward.

"Are you going to tell me why you camped out in my bell tower?" she asked. "I heard you climbing up here. Figured I'd let you rest and deal with you come sun up."

She still leaned over him, her weight resting on one hand, her beautiful face and body inches away. He wanted to hold her. Kiss that torturous mouth again. Take her until he forgot about the danger descending.

Instead, he told her the truth.

"Three drifters came out of the mountains this week. All died from dehydration. The third, though, gave us a warning before he passed."

Her spine stiffened. "Is that why you wanted me to lock up? Are more coming?"

He nodded and shrugged at the same time. "Sort of. It's not the drifters I fear."

"Then who? What?"

This time, *he* took *her* hand. If she fled, he wanted to hold on. "Ella, Grievers are coming."

Her face went blank, eyes lit bright with icy fear.

It was something they had in common. They'd discussed it during a couple of his library visits. At ten years old, Sam's father died in the desert as they searched for refuge. Sam watched his protector become a vicious revenant, a haunting predator hunting even his young son. The same happened to Ella. She'd endured a horde attack that took her family. She knew what danger awaited.

Chest rising and falling fast, she stood and half-stumbled to the tower railing, staring at the mountain peaks in silence. After a few moments, she faced him, arms across her middle as though she needed the embrace. A rogue tear tumbled down her cheek, but he couldn't tell if it'd been born of fear or anger.

"Why would you keep this from us?" she said.

Sam rose to meet her. "I didn't know until last night. I needed time to think. You know these people, Ella. You know some would've run if I let the news spread on its own. I couldn't risk that, not at night. We're safer here than if we turn to the desert, regardless. It's no place for us anymore."

The harsh lines of her features softened.

"I planned to send Perkins and Jed out this morning to notify everyone of a town meeting," he went on. "It's the best way to let everyone know."

She covered her mouth and looked back to the mountains, her body trembling.

Sam gripped his hat in both hands to keep from reaching out to her. "Tell me you're not considering leaving."

She turned, a look of confusion on her face. "Why would I leave?"

He struggled to find anything to say that didn't contain emotional barbs. "Because of James. Because you mourn him. Because of what Grievers did to you years ago, because of what they can do now. There's plenty of reasons."

She shook her head. "Sam. My grief left me a long time ago. My family has been gone for ages. And James? He volunteered for that expedition. Adventure meant more to him than I ever did."

He blinked through bewilderment. "Then why'd you—"

"Push you away?" She faced him square on. "Because you scare me. You make me feel things I've never felt. You make me want things I've never wanted. When you're near, I forget the rest of the world. And I still can't get past the thought of what it might do to me if I give in to these feelings and lose you."

Overwhelmed, Sam lost all inhibition. He closed in on her, wrapping an arm around her waist and pulling her to him. He tossed his hat aside and wiped another tear from her cheek. "What changed?"

"Something snapped inside me last night when I saw you. I couldn't let you go another minute not knowing how I felt. I hope you understand now."

His throat constricted. "I do."

"You're not alone," she said, wrapping her arms around his neck. "I'm not going anywhere. I have plenty of reasons to run, but I have an even bigger reason to stay."

She rose on her tiptoes and kissed him, and when he could finally pull himself away, he picked up his hat, and with Ella at his side, left to warn his people.

* * *

That evening, Sam and Ella stood on Main Street, staring at a ghost town. Sandy wind swirled down the road, its whistle punctuated and sharp in the silence, but not loud enough to mask the distant keening of the approaching horde. Earlier, Jed spotted a silvery sand cloud moving down the mountain, only it wasn't sand. It was Grievers. They would come that night; they were too close not to.

Ren approached from the Sundries, shoulders down and eyes tired. "The last of the houses are sealed," he said. He patted Sam on the shoulder and glanced at the business and merchant dwellings that now looked abandoned. "Everyone's scared to death."

They were, but none had jumped ship. Instead, much to Sam's amazement, they'd trusted him. Haven had hiding places. The desert had nothing but open sky, cruel sand, and crueler sun. And more hordes.

"Go," Sam said to his friend. "Get your girls into the cellar."

Ren moved on, but shouted, "See ya tomorrow."

Sam hoped those words held true.

With the sun dimming into a slice of copper light against the darkening skyline, Ella turned to him, a question glittering in her stormy eyes. "Stay with me?"

Relief filled him. He couldn't think of a better way to spend what might be his last night alive, but even more, he couldn't have left her had she cast him away.

She went ahead of him, leaving him alone to gather himself after such a difficult day. He didn't know what would remain of Haven come morning, so he strolled the empty streets, committing his beloved town to memory.

When he arrived at Ella's, he sealed the door and stared into the lightless room. He expected to find her waiting, that maybe they'd pile up between two shelves and read by candlelight until an attack or sunrise stopped them.

But she wasn't there.

He crept across the library and peered upstairs. A single light shone in the house, the flicker of candle flame from her second-floor loft. "Ella?"

"Up here."

Sam's heart pounded as he climbed. He hadn't had time to consider finding himself in an intimate setting with Ella. Now it seemed like another obstacle. He would sleep on the floor. In a chair. Anywhere he couldn't feel her warmth.

Sam reached the landing and turned at the newel post. Ella stood across the room in the same gown she'd worn the night before. She came to him and led him to a washstand where she'd poured a fresh basin of heated rosewater.

Her eyes met his, and without reluctance, she said, "Let me bathe you."

Sam stood still as she unbuttoned and peeled the shirt from his shoulders. She took up the washcloth, squeezed it, then began wiping him free of the dust and grime sticking to his skin after a day's work boarding houses.

His body responded to her touch—tightening, hardening, hurting. He didn't miss how slowly she moved, or the way her fingertips glided across his bare chest, his stomach, through the fine hair leading to his trousers, the way her sweet mouth parted on a long exhale, the way her eyes darkened when her fingertips grazed his belt and danced downward.

He stopped breathing. His desire was more than obvious.

Ella met his stare. "Is this okay?"

A small laugh left him. "You have no idea how okay."

She smiled at his reply and deftly set to unfastening his pants. When they fell, it took everything he had not to carry her to bed right then. The ache inside him throbbed to mind-numbing levels. She touched him, caressing and admiring, stroking him to the point of madness just before she'd retreat and do it all over again.

He could take no more. Heart hammering, he slid his hand around her waist, dipping low to grasp her and bring her against him. "Your gown."

She'd stripped him to his skin. He wanted her the same way.

Ella nodded, and Sam slid the garment off her shoulders. His gaze roamed, hungry as he'd ever been. He'd never seen anyone so stunning.

She pressed her naked body against his and marched him back until his knees hit the bed. Sam sat on the edge, Ella between his legs, hovering over him like a goddess.

She ran her fingers through his hair, and said, "Touch me."

His hands obeyed, discovering every inch of her as she kissed him, her supple mouth and wanting body annihilating his mind. He tried concentrating on her silk-soft skin, the goose bumps his caress left in its wake, the way she moaned for him when he touched her just so.

But the one thought he kept returning to was—If this were their only night, if one, or both, didn't survive, he wanted to know he'd loved her well.

Without breaking their kiss, he bore her into the soft mattress. She whimpered as he trailed his mouth down her neck, clutched handfuls of his hair as he worshipped her pink-pearled nipples, clawed his shoulders when he slid his fingers inside her. And when he tasted her, she cried out his name, as though he might save her, as though he might destroy her.

Then he was inside her, his entire body alive with the bliss of being buried within her. Again and again, he brought her to ecstasy, their bodies slick with sweat, their hearts so full there wasn't room to think about what else the night might hold.

When he tipped over the edge, he took her with him.

Time. Stood. Still.

He was aware of more than just the pleasure being wrenched from him, but of a completeness he'd never known filling him, a sense of consuming devotion.

Ella was his, and he was hers.

He might have no say in what happened to them after death, but he'd be damned if anyone or anything would steal this from them.

* * *

The first screams came after midnight.

Sam shot upright, a cold sweat breaking across his skin. The Grievers were so close.

He turned toward Ella. Their gazes met in a moment that said, *please be with me when this is over.*

Spurred by panic, they hurried into their clothes, and afterward, sat at the foot of Ella's bed. Waiting. Listening.

Sam held Ella, wishing he could shield her from the ear-splitting shrieks, but the phantoms' war cries only grew louder. Sam wondered if the townspeople could endure the wild wailing announcing the Grievers' need to claim or kill.

Soon, more screams filled the night; only they weren't the screams of the horde.

They belonged to the living.

He tried not to think about what might be happening to the families down Main, because that's where the bellowing human cries came from. But after a time, he found himself walking to a window, tempted to crack the shutters so he might see.

They quaked before he touched the window latch.

Once, twice, banging against the pane.

Before he could retreat, the shutters ripped from their hinges. He dove for Ella a second before glass exploded into the room, as though a Griever screamed shards.

Wraiths came from everywhere then, passing through walls, the floor, the ceiling, making the house swell and moan. They moved like silver shrieking wind, circling Sam and Ella in a tornadic funnel, their faces emotionless masks, their eyes and mouths abysses.

Images of the townspeople, the dead and mourning, filled Sam's mind, images of Ella and Ren, their bodies discarded like husks. He could hardly bear it. He felt the wraiths clawing at his mind for more, drawing his lifeforce from his body.

His feet were no longer on the floor. The Grievers were taking him, feeding off his greatest fears. For all his worry about Ella, he'd been the vulnerable one.

"Don't give in, Sam! Stay with me!" Ella's voice penetrated the darkness swallowing him, a light to cling to, a mighty roar from a woman defiant in the face of death.

The wraith looming over him howled at her. Sam heard a crash, as though the brunt of the scream had knocked Ella off her feet.

He couldn't help her. All he could do was stare into the cavernous black eyes of the thing about to devour him.

But it stared back.

Sam's heart cracked. He knew this Griever, knew the man it had once been.

Its name bloomed in his mind.

Father.

The wraith let out a shrill cry of recognition, a sound of deepest pain. Suddenly, the pressure expanding the Athenaeum's walls eased, and the Grievers flooded from the house.

Sam's body dropped to the floor. Ella crawled to him, thanking the universe for sparing him, sparing *them*, though the same couldn't be said for others. The Grievers only took their hunger to the next building.

The onslaught didn't end until sunrise. When the last wail sounded, and the town fell silent, Sam and Ella stepped from her ransacked library into the hazy desert morning, arm in arm. People trickled from their homes, dazed and wide-eyed, as Ren, Perkins, and Jed headed into dwellings to see who survived. Three died in the night, but the town united to rebuild in the names of the lost.

$$* * *$$

Weeks later, Sam sat in Ella's loft with his journal, reading his last entry. Ella strode up behind him and wrapped her arms around his neck.

"It is the thing we cannot see that will be our doom," she read.

He knew that more than ever now, but his loneliness and longing had faded. No longer did he dream of an end or fear it. With Ella, a long life seemed a gift instead of a burden.

He turned the journal to a fresh page, then pulled her into his lap. With mischievous intent, he slid his hand under her skirt. "Is this okay?"

She smiled so sweetly, then kissed his nose. "You have no idea how okay, Sheriff."

No, he couldn't live forever.

But now he knew how to make time stand still.

13Thirty Books

Exciting Thrillers, Heart-Warming Romance,
Mind-Bending Horror, Sci-Fantasy
and
Educational Non-Fiction

The Third Hour

The Third Hour is an original spin on the religious-thriller genre, incorporating elements of science fiction along with the religious angle. Its strength lies in this originality, combined with an interesting take on real historical figures, who are made a part of the experiment at the heart of the novel, and the fast pace that builds.

Ripper – A Love Story

"Queen Victoria would not be amused—but you will be by this beguiling combination of romance and murder. Is the Crown Prince of England really Jack the Ripper? His wife would certainly like to know... and so will you."
Diana Gabaldon, New York Times Best Selling Author

Heather Graham's Haunted Treasures

Presented together for the first time, New York Times Bestselling Author, Heather Graham brings back three tales of paranormal love and adventure.

Heather Graham's Christmas Treasures

New York Times Bestselling Author, Heather Graham brings back three out-of-print Christmas classics that are sure to inspire, amaze, and warm your heart.

Zodiac Lovers Series

Zodiac Lovers is a series of romantic, gay, paranormal novelettes. In each story, one of the lovers has all the traits of his respective zodiacal sign.

Never Fear

Shh… Something's Coming

Never Fear – Phobias

Everyone Fears Something

Never Fear – Christmas Terrors

He sees you when you're sleeping …

More Than Magick

Why me? Recent college grad Scott Madison, has been recruited (for reasons that he will eventually understand) by the wizard Arion and secretly groomed by his ostensible friend and mentor, Jake Kesten. But his training hasn't readied him to face Vraasz, a being who has become powerful enough to destroy the universe and whose first objective is the obliteration of Arion's home world. Scott doesn't understand why he was the chosen one or why he is traveling the universe with a ragtag group of individuals also chosen by Arion. With time running out, Scott discovers that he has a power that can defeat Vraasz. If only he can figure out how to use it.

Stop Saying Yes – Negotiate!

Stop Saying Yes - Negotiate! is the perfect "on the go" guide for all negotiations. This easy-to-read, practical guide will enable you to quickly identify the other side's tactics and strategies allowing you to defend yourself ensuring a better negotiation for your side and theirs.

13Thirtybooks.com
facebook.com/13thirty

Made in the USA
Middletown, DE
14 June 2018